Straight No Chaser:

The Beginning

By: Devin Nishea

Straight No Chaser: The Beginning

ISBN-13 978-1539897255

ISBN-10 1539897257

Edited by: Literacy Moguls, Dr. Shekina Moore

Cover Design and Book format: Brian Hamilton

I dedicate this book to my munchkin, my Boop, my heartbeat, my "why"...

Alanaa Nicole

Baby, know the sky is the limit and that you can do ALL things through Christ!

I also dedicate this book to my first love, and now, my heavenly angel—my daddy. Thank you, Daddy, for everything you showed me through your actions.

Straight No Chaser: The Beginning

Straight No Chaser: The Beginning

Chapter 1

As I lie on the bed in pain I couldn't help but to think a little piece of my life, I would never get back. In pain, thoughts of not being enough swirled through my mind. *Will I ever be married? Will I bounce back from what seems like a set back? Will I ever get over this shame I've endured?*

****

"Okay, here comes another! Okay, sweetie, I need you to push," Dr. Sharon said.

I pushed as hard as I could. Here I was bringing a life into this world, single, scared and feeling so…I don't even know the word—Ahh, yes…ALONE!! The worst feeling in the world is to be surrounded by people but yet feel so friggin' alone.

I felt more uncomfortable pressure. Oh, God…another contraction.

"Okay, sweetie, I need you to push," said Dr. Sharon.

When is this child going to be out of me!? I hadn't had anything to eat since Saturday morning and it was now late Saturday night going into Sunday morning. I had been contracting since 5 AM Friday! This little guy needed to come ON!

Straight No Chaser: The Beginning

"Okay, the next contraction, I need you to give me a big push, sweetheart," Dr. Sharon said.

"Oh, God! Can I please push NOW?" I screamed.

Contracting and being in labor for that long had taken a toll on my body and, more importantly, my friggin' patience. I was beyond ready to hold what I knew was going to be the cutest, most adorable baby in the world.

"Go ahead and push when you're ready," Dr. Sharon agreed.

That was it. I had no more left in me. I thought the actresses on TV were exaggerating. I was exhausted and I was tired of people in my personal space.

Luckily, with that last push, my child was now here. As soon as he was out, the nurses took him to clean him off. And just like that, my help, the ones holding my hands, left to go see him. I was already being ignored and it hadn't even been a whole minute, yet! All I could do was laugh to myself.

The nurses brought this perfect child to me and put him in my arms. I couldn't believe it.

I. Was. Somebody's MAMA!

Wow, and just to think, months prior I didn't know if I even wanted to be somebody's mama. But here I was, holding this pale, green-eyed baby that I was supposed to take care of for the rest of my life. I couldn't believe it. He was perfect, and I know every mama says it, but my child

really was the most handsome baby...ever! Hands down.
Everyone in the waiting room was made aware of his debut
and was excited to see him—but they had to wait. Man,
was I exhausted! And hungry!

After getting me into another room, the nursing staff
brought an unappetizing frozen dinner for me to eat. After
bonding with the baby, I eventually drifted off to sleep with
1,000 visits from the nursing staff checking on me
throughout the night.

The next morning the baby was rolled back into my room, a
little earlier than I thought.

This ended sleep as I knew it.

This day was going to prove challenging for me. I knew
the room was going to see a lot of traffic, especially after
everyone got out of church. Not only that, I was going to
have to try and breast feed. Ouch. After the nurse got the
baby in the room, she left! I was shocked. I thought she was
going to stick around; I didn't know what I was doing!
Luckily, he didn't cry.

The baby's aunts were the first visitors of the day. What I
didn't realize until after the baby was born, was that I had
to have an episiotomy. Looking back, I'm glad they didn't
tell me while it was happening. I probably would've
freaked out, and rightfully so. After having it, it made me
feel like everything was going to fall out of me (Gross!), as
I was getting up to walk to the bathroom. As the nurse was
walking with me to the restroom I couldn't help but feel a

little embarrassed. Although not even 24 hours ago, I had what seemed like a thousand people in my vajayjay.

Just as I thought, the day was busy and later that evening, I was exhausted again after all the visitation from family members and friends.

Soon enough, came the time for me to go home—thank God! I couldn't wait to get back to my bed, my pillows, my bathtub, and my wash cloths. Just *my* stuff. Next, came the realest tests of my life. *Would I be a good parent? With everything I'd gone through to bring this child into the world, would I be able to provide for him the way I wanted and needed to?*

Welp, we were about to see—ready or not!

All of this anxiety inside of one person should be illegal.

Tonight was going to be my first night by myself, at home with the most adorable baby ever. And, yes, I was scared.

But, um…

I guess, by now, you're wondering where my munchkin's father was? Well…with his wife!

This can't be my life.

Chapter 2

18 months prior

I was out shopping one day, for shoes of course, and as I was coming out of my favorite shoe store, I wasn't paying attention and I bumped into a person. "Oh my gosh I'm so sorry," I said as I was getting myself together. He looked at me and, as we locked eyes, he said, "no problem at all."

"Oh my gosh, are you ok? I wasn't paying attention, I have a lot on my mind and here I am about to take you out," I rambled. I can't even begin to tell you what I was talking about.

He interrupted me, "Ma'am, ma'am…hey, it's ok. No damage was done, we're good." he said.

Once I slowed down and looked at him…I mean really looked at him, I saw how handsome he was. I mean that grown man handsome, that I'm about my business handsome. His skin was a nice smooth milk chocolate, his teeth were so white and straight and his smile…OH MY GOSH. His smile!

After my quick survey of him I said, "Oh, okay, good. Well, have a nice day!" I walked on, in search of my next store. As I walked away, I couldn't help but take a glimpse back at him; I smiled, he was still there standing, watching me walk away. I quickly turned around before I bumped into someone or something else, and disappeared into another store.

Straight No Chaser: The Beginning

After a long day of shopping, I called a girlfriend of mine to meet for dinner and drinks; my girl, Amy.

Amy and I met in college our freshman year during summer orientation. We immediately hit it off. For me that was a great thing because none of my friends from my high school attended the college that I chose to attend. This girl had seen the good, bad and the absolute ugly of my life. But, we still remained friends over the years!

By the time I got to the restaurant, she was already there waiting for me. "Hey girl, the traffic out there was crazy! What's going on!? What did you do today," I asked as I hugged her.

"Girl, after my date last night I went home and crashed. When I finally woke up…" Amy said. I had to interrupt because Amy doesn't really date.

"Oh…wait a minute, miss girl…date? You…went on a date and you were just going to skate right on over that sentence like you didn't even say anything? No ma'am, so who'd you go out with?" I asked.

"Girl, you so dang nosey and I didn't even mean for that information to slip out!" she admitted.

"Welp, ya said it now, sooooo, spill it Lucy Pearl!" I exclaimed.

Amy had finally accepted the date of this nice-looking man that had been pursuing her for a while. I told her she was crazy for not going out with him months prior.

Come to find out, this man was a Financial Analyst for a Fortune 500 company. I have to admit, I didn't know what a Financial Analyst did or was, but it sounded important and like they made a lot of money!

"Girl, he was so dang boring, I literally almost fell asleep at the table while we were eating." she said disappointingly.

I laughed because of the facial expressions she made. "Oh girl," I said laughing. "I'm sorry it didn't go like you thought, sweetie. But, hey, at least you got your butt out of the house, right!?"

"I guess, but dannnggggg... is it too much to ask to make me laugh? Tell me a joke, do something, say something stupid for me to laugh at? I do it all the time." she said frustratingly.

"I know how you feel. Dating is not my favorite thing, but if we want to be married one day, unfortunately, we have to go through the duds." I told her.

The waiter brought out our food and drinks. After the week I had, I ordered an Old Fashioned to hit the spot; and boy did it.

After catching up with Amy and after my third Old Fashioned, she tilted her head and said, "Ok I've tried ignoring it, but this is your third drink. What's going on?" she demanded.

I hesitated, "It's over. Me and Jake. We. Are. Over. I gave myself one week to have a pity party then I could get up, dust myself off and move forward. Today is day 4. Did a little shopping, now, a little drinking. Girl, I'm good." I reassured her.

"You're over? What? What happened?" Amy asked.

"I thought we were good. Until I started noticing the little things he used to do, he wasn't doing anymore. The cute little texts, the way he stroked my hair, it all stopped and I couldn't figure it out. Then the calls started to get less and less. So, I got fed up, of course, and asked him to come over one night... and asked him what was up. And that's when he told me that he'd met someone else and he didn't want us anymore." I explained.

"What did you say?" Amy asked.

"Girl, all I could say was say, 'ok'. I couldn't deal and instead of cheating why didn't he just tell me what was up? I mean, I give you two years of my life, swerving guys every other day and for what, for my man? Girl, I'm...," I paused.

"You're what?" Amy asked.

"Never mind, I was about to say I was done with men, but that's the alcohol trying to talk." as we both laughed. We talked more so I could sober up. As we waited for our cars from valet, we hugged and parted ways.

As I got in my car, I felt a huge weight had been lifted off my shoulders. Nothing like a night with your girl, just talking and catching up and laughing 'til your abs hurt.

Straight No Chaser: The Beginning

I pulled into the drive way of my house and I couldn't wait to get inside, take a shower and finish unwinding from the day.

I walked into the house to an apple cinnamon vanilla type aroma. I bought this air freshener as a test and, surprisingly, it smelled pretty good.

I took off my heels at the door and proceeded to check the house to make sure I was the only one inside. I walked into the kitchen to see what wines I had in the fridge already chilled. Nothing I wanted, so I grabbed the bottle of whiskey a friend of mine shipped from Seattle and poured a glass and proceeded to my room.

I picked up my cell phone and, as much as I wanted to call Jake, I decided against it. Instead I sent Amy a text letting her know I made it home safely. I put my phone on silent and just laid across the bed staring at the ceiling. Then I felt a tear roll down the side of my face. Then, I felt another tear roll down the other side of my face. I was upset all over again and my tears threw me back into reality. I was thinking about life again. I was single again and had to readjust, *again*, to the single life.

This man was my world and I loved him with every ounce of me and now he was gone. No more hand-holding; no more cooking dinner and cuddling on the couch for a movie; no more bae-cations. Just no more anything! Table for one was all I was hearing now. Wow, it was so easy for him to just pick up and leave. What was wrong with me that made him leave? Did I not talk enough? Did I gain weight? Did I not love him enough?

These questions and more rushed through my head again, for the umpteenth time that week. I finally pulled myself off the bed after lying there for two hours. I picked up my whiskey and took a sip and, as it hit the back of my throat, I closed my eyes and took another sip. I got up off the bed, walked into the bathroom to take a shower. I undressed and got into the hot and steamy shower and it seemed as if my body melted as the hot water hit my skin. I stood under the water for what seemed like hours. I don't know what happened but the tears started flowing again. This time instead of just tears streaming my face, I started sobbing and fell to my knees in the shower and just cried it out.

I couldn't control myself and I couldn't get a grip this time. This pain right now, at this moment, I couldn't handle. I don't know how I did it, but I finished my shower and still crying, dried myself off, put my favorite robe on and sat down on my bed again. Grabbed my glass of whiskey and drank. I looked down at my phone and saw my message indicator light blinking. I picked it up and a piece of me was hoping it was a missed call from Jake, but instead, I had a text from Amy, some emails from work and a missed call from my mama. When I saw she had called I rolled my eyes and threw my phone back on the bed. I hadn't told her about the break up yet and I was not in the mood to talk to her about it yet. As a matter of fact, today was my first day out of the house other than going to work.

I'd been avoiding all phone calls, but I had to get out of the house today and feel human again. My job allowed me to work from home part of the week because of a "stomach thing" I caught. This made it easier for me to just stay home away from the real world, while I sorted through the break up. But, I didn't get it. This was the first time a break up had me like this. I mean, normally I would cry and be upset for one day and move on, but this time around...

Maybe it was because we were together so long. You know one miserable night for each year we were together. As I thought about how long we were together, I was over my allotted number of days to sulk. This was day four!

"Awe Zen girl...tonight is the LAST night for this mess!" I declared to myself. Tomorrow is a new freakin' day and you will NOT cry about this tomorrow. We're putting a stop to this right now. No, you didn't deserve what he did to you but guess what, it happened. And there's nothing you can do about it, girl. So, why are you worried?" I said out loud to myself.

As I sat on my bed with my drink in my hand, I wiped my face and searched for a movie to watch. Something funny, none of that romantic bull crap!! I went and popped some popcorn and cuddled up on my couch and watched the movie until it watched me.

Chapter 3

The light that peeked through my blinds and curtains woke me out of my sound sleep. The TV was still on from the night before and my uneaten popcorn was on the coffee table. I laid there for a while to take in my surroundings before getting up to move around. It took me a few minutes to figure out what day it was and I realized it was Sunday. After my day of drinking, I was surprised that my head wasn't being used as some band's drum line.

I sat up on the sofa and looked around the room, took in a deep breath, got up and started moving around. I cleaned up my popcorn feast from the night before, the little bit of whiskey I didn't get to drink before dozing off, I poured down the drain. I proceeded to make some coffee.

I normally attend church on Sundays, but I realized I overslept. It was already 11 AM!! I walked back to my room and spotted my phone on the bed. I kind of hated to pick it up to see what I missed Saturday night. Against my better judgment, I picked it up and there it was.

Two missed calls from mama. One text from mama and one text from Amy, one missed text from my sister and one missed call from an unknown number.

I debated listening to my voicemail. But went ahead and listened anyway. My mama was going on and on about avoiding her calls and I needed to call her back to let her know I was still in the "land of the living." The text from her said the same. All I could do was yell at my phone

Straight No Chaser: The Beginning

"I'm okay, mama. Dang!" I hung up the phone and didn't bother listening to see if I had more messages. I put the phone on the charger and started to clean. Sometimes cleaning and de-cluttering helped me through whatever I was going through. The first things that had to go…Jake's things.

I walked around the house until I found a box to put his things in. Man, as I was gathering his things I was thinking to myself, "man, I hope I don't break down again."

Thank God I didn't! I put his box of things by the door, which, to my surprise, wasn't much. He stayed at my place at least three times each week. I wasn't ready to talk to or to see him yet. So, I taped the box up. I would drop it by the post office tomorrow on my way to work.

Before going back to my cleaning, I made a cup of coffee in my favorite mug, sat at the bar in the kitchen and enjoyed the quietness of my morning. After two cups of coffee and watching my neighborhood doing some sort of exercise, I decided to get my butt up and get back to running today. After not running for a few days I knew it was going to be a tough run.

I went back to my room and changed into my running tights, made sure I put on deodorant, put on my Brooks and off I went.

Finishing up my run back to my house, I noticed a car in my driveway. I slowed up a little and braced myself for some potential foolishness. The closer I got, I saw it was my parents. "Great," I said out loud. I was not in the mood yet to deal with my mom. I hadn't gotten my story together yet on why I avoided her calls. And I'm sure she was going to have something to say about my not going to church. I ran into the driveway and saw they were still sitting in the car with the windows down and gospel music playing.

I ran to the car out of breath and said, "Hey y'all what you doing here?" Bending over trying to catch my breath.

My mama said, "Hey! Where are you coming from? Looks like you've been running. Been to church today?" Yep. She said that all in one breath!

As I sighed, "Y'all come on inside." I was trying to get myself together quickly for my mama. She has the tendency to be a bit much at times. I unlocked the door and, as we walked in, I was beyond glad I cleaned the house or else that would be something else for mama to nag me about. They sat down; my dad still hadn't really said anything other than 'hey'. I was still trying to stretch.

"Y'all want something to drink?" I asked.

"Nah, I have dinner at the house. We hadn't heard from you all week. I've called several times," my mama probed.

"Mama, I've been busy with work all week. I was working on a deadline," I stuttered.

"I told you she was probably busy with work," my dad interjected.

"Oh ok. Well are you cooking today?" she asked as she was walking about the house being nosey.

Then she spotted the box by the door. Oh hell, Jake's box! Welp, no escaping it now.

"What's that box at the door?" she asked.

"Nothing mama. So what have y'all been up to this week?" I quickly changed the subject.

My dad spoke up, and said, "I've done nothing all week really, went to visit some people in the hospital. I cooked dinner the other night."

My mom interrupted, "Yep, he cooked fish & hushpuppies. It was good. I tried to call you over. Everybody was asking about you."

"Oh really, like who?" I asked with a deep sigh.

"Well, you didn't answer your phone so it doesn't really matter now, does it?" she said sarcastically.

I looked at my dad and we both shook our heads.

Then the other line of questioning started. I knew it.

"So, where's Jake?" mama asked.

I didn't know if I would make it through. "Um, not sure about today, but we may get up with each other later." I said. I tried not to make eye contact with her.

"What do you mean you don't know where he is, you're supposed to know!" she looked suspicious.

Straight No Chaser: The Beginning

"Ma, it's ok. So, what did you cook for dinner?" I asked. The house phone rang as soon as I asked, thank GOD!

"Hello? Oh hey, I'm well how are you? Yes...ok...ok...ok that sounds good, just give me a call on your way. Ok, it was good to hear from you too. Ok, bye-bye," I ended the conversation.

I returned to the living room with my parents. My mom said, "Ok, well, we're getting ready to go home."

"Ok, thanks for stopping by to check on me," I said.

"Mmmmhmmm, you're welcome, baby. Well, we'll see ya later," my mom said.

I walked them to the car, hugged them and saw them on their way. I stayed outside until the car was out of site.

I walked back into the house to finish cleaning up and to find something to eat. After my run I was starving! I walked into the kitchen and started to nibble on last night's dessert.

I didn't eat all of it because I wanted to save some for later and I'm glad I did! As I was nibbling, I was thinking back to my mama's line of questioning. Lord knows I love my mama, but sometimes, she is a bit much. Had the phone not rang, I'm sure she would've started asking me about when Jake and I were going to get married. Ugh!

I walked into my room, A.K.A. the war room, and the light of day exposed the state I had been in all week. Clothes were everywhere; an empty bottle of wine was on the nightstand, a whiskey glass, uneaten popcorn. I don't make it a habit of eating in my bedroom, but this week was the exception to the rule. Candy wrappers were everywhere, Coke Zero bottles, yeah I was in bad shape. I turned my gospel music on full blast and stripped my bed, washed my depressed sheets and towels, cleaned my bathroom, washed clothes and put the things I bought the day before away.

After I showered and dressed, my starvation level was at the max. So, the mission was to get to somebody's brunch and bottomless mimosas immediately. I called my girl Amy to tag along, but she had already eaten. Everybody I called had eaten.

I grabbed a book and went by myself. Since it was nice outside I sat outside on the patio to enjoy the view of the lake and read my book.

As I was enjoying the view of the lake and watching the boats cruise slowly as they docked, I reflected on how blessed my life was. I smiled as I took a deep breath to take in the fresh air.

I scanned the patrons and everyone looked like they were having the greatest day and they had no problems, no drama in their lives. But I knew better than anyone that right under the surface is where all the drama occurs.

I enjoyed my food, mimosas and book. After reading and people-watching I needed to leave and get to my next stop, which I hadn't figured out yet.

As I was leaving I looked closer towards the water and saw the same guy I bumped into while shopping. I smiled and left immediately.

Chapter 4

"Okay, guys, great job on the Holly Fields account. So far they are impressed by our work and attention to their account," I told my team on our daily conference call.

"Zen, are they looking into a holiday campaign? If so, we may need to go ahead and get some ideas down and ready to present," Bob said.

"Yes, Bob, that was actually next on the agenda to talk about. The holidays are not that far away but, yet, around the corner. You guys get together, start your brainstorming process and we'll reconvene," I told them.

I ended the call the way I always do, "alright guys go out there and make it happen. Thank you so much for your hard work on this account. Things are really starting to look up for our new business side. Make it great day," as I disconnected from the conference call.

It had been a month since my mini-breakdown and I was finally starting to feel like myself again, thank God. I was paying better attention to the words coming out of my mouth and how could I forget about my appearance? My game had stepped back up! I knew it would take some time but dang, I didn't know it would take that long! I was in a good place, still missed Jake, but in a good place. I still hadn't called him, which was great. After I mailed him his things, he tried to reach out to me but I never answered his calls and, eventually the calls stopped.

Straight No Chaser: The Beginning

"Zen, you have a visitor here to see you; would you like for me to send them in," my assistant said.

I looked at her with a side eye and said, "Umm, did I overlook a meeting today or someone's popping up?" I asked.

She came inside my office and closed the door, which made me a little nervous. My first thought was, "Awe hell, what?"

Although I hadn't shared with anyone about my break up, she knew something was up. Jake and I met for lunch weekly and I took that off my calendar and she hadn't seen him so I knew she knew.

She walked closer to my desk and said hesitantly, "Jake's here."

The sound of his name made me stop cold in my tracks. I completely lost my train of thought and stared at her, my eyes like daggers.

"Oh really?" I asked trying to get myself together. "Tell him I'm busy and I'll have to call him later." I told her.

"I've already done that, but he insists on waiting until you finish what you're doing." she said.

"Shit," I said. "Welp, tell him again, I'm busy and I don't know how long I'm going to be because I'm swamped." I demanded.

She let out a deep sigh and said, "Ok." She disappeared behind the closed door to deliver the news.

Straight No Chaser: The Beginning

I thought to myself, "What the ham does he want? I can NOT with him today. The nerve of him..." My thoughts were cut off by picking up the phone.

The phone rang and before the person on the other end could say anything, I interjected.

"Can you believe this fool stopped by my office unannounced a few minutes ago!?" I yelled. "Unannounced! What is wrong with him?" I asked.

"Zen, calm down girl. Take a breath and step away from the ledge." Amy urged.

I did what she instructed.

She let out this little laugh, "Hmph, so he stopped by? What did he say?" she asked.

"He didn't say anything. I told my assistant to tell him I was going to be tied up all day." I told her. "Girl, I'm not ready to see or talk to him yet. I was doing good until this; I bet he came by here unannounced on purpose just to piss me off!" I exclaimed.

"Zen, we don't know that. But if he did want to piss you off, he kinda succeeded," Amy pointed out.

"Why don't you see what he wants, didn't you say he called you last month?" Amy asked.

"Yep." I said abruptly.

"Well honey, maybe he wants to try to work things out." Amy said slowly.

"Amy, there's no working anything out right now. He tells me he was pretty much cheating on me for a year, left me to be with her; girl NO!" I said.

"I understand but I do think you should reach out to him to see what he wants. Maybe not today, but sometime soon." she said.

"Hmph, we'll see." I said and hung up the phone.

I buzzed my assistant back into my office.

"Have a seat Sarah. Okay, I need you to listen to me carefully. Let me preface this by saying you did nothing wrong. But, if Jake comes by or calls, you are to tell him I am either not here or tied up. He is not to come into my office for any reason. If he needs to leave something for me he can do so with you. If I am roaming the office and he's here, text me to let me know when he leaves. This goes unless I tell you otherwise," I said sternly.

I hated putting her in the middle of this drama, but it was necessary at the moment and I didn't see any other way out.

"Yes ma'am," Sarah said with a shaking voice. "Umm, can I assume you two are no longer?" she asked.

"Bold of you to ask, but, yes, you can assume that." I responded.

"Ok, well he did leave some very pretty flowers for you; I'll bring them in." she said.

Before I had the chance to say anything she had disappeared into the lobby. She came back in with a bouquet of my favorite flowers; white roses and Cala Lilies.

I cleared my throat, "Thanks...you can sit them wherever."

As I was sitting there admiring the flowers I almost shed a tear thinking about the good times.

"Ok, there ya go, Zen, did you need me for anything else? If not I'll leave you be." she said.

I shook my head and she disappeared again behind the door. I stared at the flowers until my trance was broken. I got up to admire the flowers closer. I saw there was a card and I grabbed it, sat on the desk to read it.

Zen...I think about you every day.

I miss you, I miss us.

Love always,

Jake

You miss me? You miss us!? Dude, puhleeze. You had me in your space and you decided to stray away because you thought the grass was greener somewhere else. I took the flowers to Sarah and told her she could have them, placed them on her desk and went back into my office for rest of the day, uninterrupted. I kept the card.

After the day I had, I couldn't wait to get home and unwind. So I wouldn't lag behind, as soon as I got home I changed into my running tights, laced up my Brooks and I ran...and ran...and ran until I couldn't run anymore. I kinda felt like Forest Gump. Running normally cleared my head and it did just that tonight.

After I got back home I stretched in the drive way and jumped some rope before I called it a night with my workout. I showered and cooked a healthy dinner; salmon and asparagus and it was oh so good after the workout I had. As I was eating dinner and watching TV, my doorbell rang. I looked at my phone to see what time it was; 8:24pm, then I glanced back at my door. I wasn't expecting anyone to stop by and I hated unannounced visitors. I couldn't *not* answer the door because whoever it was saw my lights were on. The doorbell rang again, now for the third or fourth time. I decided to ignore it. If someone called me out about it, I decided I was going to tell them I was in the shower or something. The doorbell stopped ringing and I heard the car door shut, the car started up again. I looked at my phone waiting for it to ring and nothing. I waited for a text and nothing. Now I was curious to know who it was. I didn't want to risk the chance of opening the door and it being Jake. I still wasn't ready. After eating and watching TV I decided to call Amy and report what happened earlier.

The phone rang and rang then went to voicemail. Funny that rarely happens. I'll just catch up with her later.

I rifled through my purse and pulled out the card Jake left with the flowers. I read it again.

As crazy as it sounds, to read the card hurt but it also made me feel closer to him somehow. And I missed him, too. I looked at the card until I drifted off to sleep.

Chapter 5

"Hello?" I answered.

"Hi, may I speak to Xenia," the male voice inquired. I know this was someone I hardly ever spoke with. No one called me by my real name.

"Umm, yes, speaking. Who's calling, please?" I asked.

"Oh, yeah, this is Robert, Amy's friend. She passed me your number. Please tell me she let you know I was going to call?" he asked.

I let out a deep sigh, "Yes, she did let me know. Um, how are you?"

"Oh, good, this is already a bit awkward enough," he confirmed. Awkward it was.

After recovering from the break up, Amy took it upon herself to try and set me up with someone to get me out of the house again.

"Yep, it sure is and I'm glad I'm not the only one who thinks so," I answered. To answer your question, I'm fine," I said.

"I'm sorry I didn't ask, but are you busy, is this a good time?" he asked.

This was a great out for me but before I could say I was busy, my mouth opened and said, "Oh no, no this a great time."

FACE PALM! Oh, Zen, get it together, girl.

"By the way, everyone calls me Zen," I told him.

"Well, Zen, nice to meet your acquaintance, although over the phone," he laughed.

A little corny, but that was cool because I'm corny too.

Robert and I talked for about an hour, getting to know each other. I couldn't help but feel like we were on an interview. Everything seemed so formal. But we decided to meet for coffee Saturday morning at the local coffee shop on the other side of town. I didn't want to meet anywhere close to my house, just in case. You can never be too careful. I'm sure he was thinking the same.

As soon as we hung up, I called Amy to give her a little piece of my mind.

As soon as she answered the phone she says, "So how'd the conversation go?"

I rolled my eyes at the phone and answered, "Thanks for the heads up chick! He caught me totally off guard."

"Yeah, I told you I was going to give him your number," she said.

"Yeah, but you didn't tell me when so I could prep myself for his phone call," I replied.

"Okay, well, whatever... what did you think of Robert?" Amy probed.

"He seemed okay, but we're meeting at Black Bean Saturday for coffee," I told her.

"Black Bean? That's across town, why so far?" she asked.

"Well, we don't know each other, so I didn't want to choose a place close to the house in case he's a little crazy," I said laughingly.

"Understood. Well, I can assure you he's not crazy. Well, I hope it works out, but if not it's cool, he's just one cool person that you've met so far. And you need to get out there and mingle my dear," she said.

"Yeah I know, but I hate starting over, Amy," I said.

"I know it sucks, but, girl, dating is a numbers game and the quicker you get through the duds, the quicker you can get to Mr. Right. Right!? So, pep up, Pippy. You'll be okay. You just needed a nudge," she said laughing.

I knew she was right and it had been months since Jake and I had broken up so I "womaned up" and took that step forward.

Saturday morning came way too quickly. I had some time before meeting Robert, so I decided to go for a run. I got in a few miles then got ready to leave the house for my coffee "date."

I pulled up to Black Bean early and hyped myself up before getting out of the car. I looked in my mirror to make sure my make-up was okay, retouched my favorite lipstick and off I went. Although this was a casual thing, I still wanted to look my absolute best. So, of course, I pulled out my heels, pair of boyfriend jeans and oversized button down. I looked good, I felt good.

I walked inside the coffee shop, ordered an extra hot caramel latte and grabbed a table. Amy sent me a picture of Robert the night before so I'd know what he looked like. I arrived maybe ten minutes before our scheduled time. I sat at the table positioned so I could see him when he walked in. Our scheduled time came and went. Amy just so happened to text me as I was about to text her, to see how things were going.

Hey girl, just checking to see how things are going.

I simply responded,

I'd be able to tell you if he were here!

My phone rang and I picked up on the first ring.

"He's not there?" Amy sounded pissed.

"Nooope. Not yet. We agreed on 11am. It's been 20 minutes and I'm trying my best to give him the benefit of the doubt," I told her.

"Um, yeah, I understand all of that, but either way he's late and it doesn't sound like he's called to give you an explanation," she said.

"Nooope, he hasn't. Ten more minutes and I'm out," I said calmly.

Straight No Chaser: The Beginning

This would be the reason I hate blind dates that are set up by friends. I'm not upset with Amy about his flakiness, but she obviously thought highly of him to mention my name.

As I sat there counting down my last ten minutes, I took in the sites and aroma of the coffee shop. I loved this place because of its quaint homey atmosphere. The staff was great. I came here enough for everyone to know my name and vice versa.

When they saw me come through the door, they always knew the drink I wanted. I told them one day I was going to order something different just to trip them up. It hasn't happened yet and I said that two years ago. I looked around and saw they added new paintings by the main entrance and the patio entrance.

All of the paintings hanging were by local artists. I even bought a few for my house. What I loved most about the shop were the coffee cups. No cup was the same, some looked like antiques, some looked like fine China. I got so caught up in my surroundings, when I looked at the time it was 11:45 AM.

I finished my latte, gathered my things and left. Still no phone call or text from Robert, explaining himself by the time I walked to the car. What a waste of an outfit.

By this time I was starving, so, I decided to go to my favorite brunch spot.

I shot Amy a quick text letting her know her friend had officially stood me up. I looked up from my phone and saw this guy walking into Black Bean. As I looked closer, it

Straight No Chaser: The Beginning

looked just like the guy I literally bumped into months prior.

I said out loud, "That can't be him!" He was still as sexy as I remembered.

I started my car and proceeded to pick up something to eat. As I was driving I couldn't help but hearing my ego deflate. Really? You opt to stand me up instead of call and say that something had come up and couldn't make it?

"Jerk," I said out loud.

I pulled up to the restaurant and parked my car. I saw they were pretty busy, but hopefully there was a seat at the bar waiting for me. I glanced down at my phone and read Amy's response to Robert not showing, "Jerk!"

I laughed and proceeded to walk inside.

The hostess asked how many in my party and I asked if there was room at the bar for one. She walked over to check for me and motioned for me to come over.

As I got closer to where she was, I saw she had a place for me by another young lady.

When I took a closer look, I noticed that I knew her. I walked up behind her and said in a deep voice, "Hey, baby, is this seat taken?"

Amy flung around so fast in her chair and I yelled, "Wasssuuuuppp!" We both laughed.

"Oh, girl, you were about to be slapped!" she exclaimed.

I laughed and said, "Ha! Yeah-yeah."

We hugged and sat down together and the hostess left us alone.

"Well funny running into you here!" I was really excited to see her.

"I know right. Listen, I'm sorry about Robert. I'm so pissed with him right now," Amy said.

"Well, it's not cool, but it's cool." I responded. My ego is a little bruised but I'm good."

"And he still hadn't called you to explain?" she inquired.

"Nope. Okay, let's not talk about him," I begged.

The bartender took our drink orders as we looked over the menu. By the time our bartender brought us our first mimosa, we ordered our food.

"So, miss girl," I said. "What's been going on with you, since you know all of my business?" We both laughed.

"Well, I got a promotion that was finalized on Thursday!" Amy exclaimed.

"Girl, get out of here! Congratulations! Raise your glass." I said as we toasted to her success.

"And the guy I went out with a few months ago, the one you couldn't believe I went out with. Well, it looks like it's getting more serious," Amy said.

Straight No Chaser: The Beginning

I screamed, "OMG!!" I actually got up and did a happy dance for her. I laughed, the bartender laughed. I asked the bartender for another mimosa.

"Umm dancing like that miss girl, you don't need another," Amy joked.

We laughed and ate our food and talked until we were all talked out.

"So?" I asked as I placed some of my omelet in my mouth.

"So, what?" she asked.

"Tell me about this dude, let me live vicariously through your dating life." I told her as I laughed.

"Well, we both know how I am about men. I can be hard on them, I admit that, but if they can put up with all of that I know they have some substance to them," she said smiling hard.

So, I had to ask, "So, what made him so different?"

"Remember my car had broken down a few months ago and I was stressing about it? Well, he paid for the repairs. All $3,500 of it! I didn't ask him to do it, didn't hint to him *anything*. He didn't flinch, whipped out the checkbook and BAM! Plopped it on the table like he had just won a Spades game. And when I tried paying him back he wouldn't accept it. Not only that, he goes with me to church and prays for me and *with* me," she shook her head in amazement.

Straight No Chaser: The Beginning

I was so happy for my friend for opening up and allowing love to flow. I'd been waiting for this moment for her for so long!

I looked at her and said, "Awe, look at you blushing. I don't think I've seen you blush before. Oh my god, I'm so happy for you."

"I am happy, Zen! So far, he has exceeded my expectations, but the relationship is still new, so I'm still a little cautious," she said.

"Okay, okay…I understand. Bartender! Another mimosa, please. So, are you guys going out tonight?" I asked.

"Yeah, he's coming over for dinner and a movie," she said smiling.

By this time, we had been sitting at the bar for three hours! And our bottomless mimosas—yeah, we were working on our fourth one. I asked the bartender for coffee so I could sober up before driving myself home. I excused myself to the restroom.

When I walk in I overhear two girls talking in the stalls. That's always awkward when I walk in and hear conversations going. Well, one girl was talking about how she had a feeling her boyfriend was cheating on her.

"Girl, how do you figure he's cheating?" one of the girls asked.

"Because I read his text messages last night and one of the messages said how she was looking forward to tomorrow, and she enjoyed talking to him on the phone the other night," the other girl replied.

I stopped in my tracks. I washed my hands quickly and, staggered my way back to Amy.

I looked Amy dead in her face.

"Well, I know why your boy was a no show today. He has a girl!" I said.

Amy looked at me confused and said, "Huh?"

"Yep, overheard two girls talking about how she thought her man was cheating and how she read a text last night from another girl about meeting today and how she enjoyed speaking with him the other night on the phone," I said.

Before she could even say anything, I whipped out my phone and let her read our messages.

"Oh, my god, Zen, I swear I didn't know, I…" Amy said

I cut her off mid-sentence, "Hey, I know you wouldn't do anything like that to me let alone anyone else."

"Man, wait until I speak to him." Amy said infuriated. Oh, let me call him now," she said.

Her call went to voicemail, of course.

"Hey Robert, it's Amy. Listen, I was calling to see how it went this morning with Zen. I hope all went well. I hadn't heard from her yet and, since I'm talking to your voicemail,

I'm hoping you two are together! Give me a call," she said sweetly.

After she hung up, we both looked at each other and said, "Jerk," and exploded in laughter.

Chapter 6

Some time passed and the dating scene was getting tired. I started coming across the same guys, just different names. So I took this time to make sure I was working on me before jumping into a relationship. One night while I was sitting in the quietness and stillness of the evening on my patio with my glass of wine, I realized I was trying to mask my pain and heartache with someone else instead of healing my heart first. Simple, yet profound. I couldn't believe something so simple could literally change my life. I couldn't just let my work consume me and think I was healing.

At that very moment I went into the house, found an empty journal and pen and perched on the patio and began to write. I didn't have anything in particular to write about.

I knew I needed to rearrange my life, so I simply asked myself, "What makes Zen happy?"

After sitting in the lounge chair for fifteen minutes, unable to think of one thing, I knew there was a problem.

Not one thing? This revealed to me that, in my relationships, I only catered to his needs and happiness. Not good. So, I began to think about the things I used to do, that brought me genuine joy and laughter to my soul and life. I realized this was it, "operation get your life back." I was a little excited about it, to be completely honest. All this time I think I conformed to how everyone around me wanted me to live my life, instead of sticking to my convictions and doing what I knew would make me happy. The more I thought about it, the more it overwhelmed me a little. I had to undo all of these years and start from scratch. It can't be done overnight but it will be done.

So, where do I start? I decided to start with "me time." That's the only way I saw myself *getting back to me*. But I didn't want to completely cut people out of my life in the process, because, truth be told, I could be by myself—all day, everyday!

"Maybe that's what I need to do. Cut out the distractions; just me and God," I thought to myself. If I have outside distractions it could hinder what I'm trying to do."

By this time I was pacing around my house, with my journal in hand. This thing became attached to my hip. I always had it with me in case I became inspired, wanted to jot down an idea or two. I became a professional journal-er. If that's a word! I laughed out loud at myself.

I read back over some things I had previously written down. And on the top of one of the pages, I had written "FEARS" in capital letters. On the lines below it, the first on my list was a fear of heights. Then I asked myself, "How are you going to get over this?" I'd flown in a plane hundreds of times for both business and pleasure, and still… scared. I'd even sit in the window seat and I'd still be scared. I laughed at myself again.

I had this bright idea and ran to my laptop, opened it and began to do a search for races. I thought I could knock some things out quickly in one full swoop.

Straight No Chaser: The Beginning

I found the race I heard so much about from my run group. There, I did it. I signed up for a half marathon on the coast that would include running over a 2-mile bridge with tons of flowing water underneath.

As soon as I pressed submit, I said out loud, "What the hell did I just do!?" Oh my god, I have a fit driving over bodies of water, now I just decided to RUN over a body of water!? Great, good job Zen. Never mind the fact that I've never run a half marathon before. Good thing I was already in pretty good running shape because the race would be in two months.

After sitting at my desk for what seemed like an eternity, I moved myself to the kitchen to feed my face. I felt myself beginning to stress and that's not what I needed or wanted. But I grabbed the bag of chips anyway...and cookies...and soda.

After a full day of brunching, boozing and shopping, I decided to stop by a local bakery to pick up one of my favorite cheesecakes, maple glaze! On a Saturday afternoon I was expecting a mad house. But, to my surprise, it wasn't that busy. For that I was thankful because I was in a hurry to get home to do absolutely nothing in front of my TV, on the couch with a nice glass of wine. Not to mention I was tired beyond belief. After the early morning blind date debacle, I just wanted to unwind. I still could not believe this dude stood me up. I'm not even sure if he had returned Amy's call. Eh well. I checked my hair, make-up and nose before getting out of the car to head into the bakery.

Straight No Chaser: The Beginning

"Man, my feet are killing me," I said out loud. I guess that's what I get for wearing brand new heels all day. I normally put an extra pair of shoes in my car but of course not today! But hey, they were cute.

I finally made it to the door of the bakery. The girl behind the counter looked up and saw it was me and we exchanged smiles.

"Heeey, Zen!" she said with excitement. Long time, no see. Where have you been?" she inquired.

"Hey, sweetie! I know, I know. I had to cut back, I was coming in here way too much and was about to spoil this figure I worked so hard to get," I said as we both laughed.

This is the bakery I always came to when Jake and I were together. I was honestly hoping I wasn't going to run into him or be asked about him.

"Well, where's that handsome man of yours?" she asked.

Yep, spoke too soon.

"Well, we're no longer together," I replied.

She looked crushed, "Awe, I'm sorry to hear that."

"Oh, it's okay, things happen," I replied, quickly changing the subject. "Okay, so, you know what I came for—maple-glaze me!" I said.

She disappeared behind the door leading into the kitchen. I gave the room a quick scan to see who was in my vicinity.

Straight No Chaser: The Beginning

I saw him. The guy I kept bumping into around town. I froze in the place I was standing and just stared at him, taking him in from head to toe. He was still as handsome as I remembered. Then…he looked up and we locked eyes. Dang it, I didn't know what to do. Do I wave? Do I smile? Do I go over and introduce myself? Oh, my GOD! He's getting up. By this time, Lydia had come back with my cheesecake. I turned around quickly.

"Okay, Ms. Zen! The maple glaze was just made fresh for you, love," she said as she was ringing up my order. I was so nervous I was shaking because I didn't know if handsome was coming my way or not.

I pulled my wallet out of my purse to pay Lydia, just for it to drop on the floor by accident. As I was reaching down for it, I see a hand touch it and a voice say "No, no, let me get that for you." We locked eyes and I smiled.

"Thanks," I said shyly.

"No problem," he said, simply, as he placed the wallet in my hand.

As I was taking the money out to pay Lydia, she then says, "Because I know you so well, I placed a car slice in the bag for you."

My eyes lit up, "Oh, Ms. Lydia, you are the best! Thank you so much. And, yes, you know I will sit in my car and eat it." We all laughed. I turned and Handsome was still standing there, smiling.

"Hi. Thanks again for getting my wallet for me," I said.

Straight No Chaser: The Beginning

"Like I said, no problem, it was my pleasure. You must be a regular, as well, if Ms. Lydia's hooking you up with a car slice," he joked.

I couldn't help but stare. His eyes. His voice. His lips. Whew!

I broke out of my trance and said, "Oh, um, yeah, but I haven't been in here in awhile. Trying to watch what I eat."

Lydia was still standing at the counter grinning from ear to ear, listening to our conversation.

"You look great. I mean…yeah, you look great," he said smiling and doing that LL Cool J-lick'n- his-lips thing. OH MY GOD!!!

"Jesus!" I exclaimed. I couldn't believe I said that out loud.

"What's wrong?" he asked.

"Oh, Jesus, look at the time." I tried to recover from my outburst. I gotta go, I'm running late." I said.

"Okay, well don't let me hold you up. My name's Isaiah, by the way," he says extending his hand.

I glanced down at his hand and grabbed it. I looked at him for a few seconds, second-guessing if I should share my name.

"Xenia. Nice to meet you, Isaiah," I finally replied.

Straight No Chaser: The Beginning

I grabbed my cheesecake Lydia had placed in a bag for me and walked toward the door.

My entire body tensed up walking away because I knew he was still standing there watching me walk away. The entire time I'm praying to God, begging him not to let me fall or slip. I finally made it to the door and wanted to turn around so badly. I turned around and pushed the door open with my back and glanced up...he was gone!

I laughed at myself as the door shut. I wanted to run to my car, bad, but, number 1, my feet still hurt and, number 2, a sure way for me to fall, was to run.

I kept my cool until I sat in the car. I began talk to myself, "Oh, my God, I just knew he was still looking at me walk away. I am so embarrassed. But it's about time I finally met him after seeing him around these past few months."

All of this while I'm stuffing my face with cheesecake. I'm not sure what was different or if it had been that long since I'd eaten a slice but this cheesecake was extra good today! I closed my eyes as I savored another bite.

"His name is Isaiah. Oh, fine Isaiah has a firm handshake. Maybe I should have given him my number? Hmph, this cake is good!" I exclaimed.

As I finished up my car slice, I started my car so I could get home and relax. On my way home, I thought about the events of the day. The way my day is ending is surely different than how it started. I had almost forgotten about Robert. "Jerk," I said out loud.

I heard the notification for my phone go off. The next stop light I checked my phone. My smile became a scowl. "Oh NOW you want to text me…7 hours later!?" I screamed at the phone.

I placed my phone back into its cubby and drove home. I picked up my phone again and sent Amy the text Robert sent.

Hey I'm so sorry I was a no show this morning, but something came up last minute. I will call you later this evening if that's ok? I know you're probably upset with me. I'd like to make it up to you.

After I got home, I devoured half of my sweet treat and dozed off watching movies.

Chapter 7

After an exhausting day of work, I decided to treat myself to dinner. I liked this *getting back to me* thing. I loved just spending time with me and loving on me for once.

"Table for 1 please, or, if I could just sit at the bar, that would be great," I told the hostess.

She escorted me to the bar area to be seated.

"Here you go ma'am," she said politely as I sat down.

I melted into the seat as the bartender came to take my drink order.

"Hey beautiful what ya drinking tonight?" he asked. He had the most gorgeous smile.

"Yeah, umm, whiskey sour please, light on the ice." I told him. As he made my drink I sat there with my eyes closed for a few seconds, just taking in the sound of the bar. There was some kind of game playing on the television— not sure which sport and, at that point, I couldn't care less.

The bartender brought my drink back and sat it down in front of me.

"Are we eating tonight or just drinking?" he asked.

"Oh man I hadn't even looked at the menu yet, I'm sorry." I said.

"Oh no, take your time and I'll be back," he winked at me before walking away.

This low key "play flirting" is what I needed as I smiled at him.

After talking with the bartender I found out his name was Brad. Brad had been working at the bar for almost a year part-time to save up to buy his girlfriend an engagement ring. He told me all about their whirlwind affair of how they met to present day.

"Here's your dinner love, enjoy." he said as he turned to check on the other patrons at the bar.

This was my first time at this bar and the food was great. Not the typical food you'd expect in a bar. I had the best Duck Confit and it was cooked perfectly. This place reminded me of one of the places you would see on Diners, Drive Ins and Dives on the Food Network. I raved so much about the Duck, the bartender brought the chef out to meet me.

"Thank you so much ma'am, it's my pleasure," he said.

"Well, this is my first time here but it will definitely not be my last!" I assured them.

This was honestly going to be one of my happy hour spots and I couldn't wait to tell Amy!

To my surprise, the chef sent out one of his specialty desserts. Although I didn't know the name of it, it was light tasting; he sealed the deal with this chocolate decadence.

After my exquisite meal, I dragged myself to the car for my drive home.

Chapter 8

I volunteered to bring pastries for my team to the morning team meeting. Of course, I was running late today. Good thing Black Bean was five minutes from work. I parked and rushed in and, yeah, of course, they were busy!

I ordered a coffee jug for the team and their homemade treats, which are to die for. I also ordered myself a white chocolate mocha to take the edge off of the morning madness.

While I waited for my order, I took in the busy sights of the morning. I decided at that moment I was going to slow down enough to enjoy the scenery.

Just then, I heard someone say, "Ma'am I have your order and I'll help you to your car."

"Oh, thanks so much," I replied.

I grabbed my mocha and he followed me out to my car. He made sure everything was secure and walked away.

As I was getting in the car, I heard someone call my name again.

"Hey, Xenia! Xenia, wait up!" the voice yelled.

I turned in all directions to see who was calling me. It was Mr. Tall, Chocolate and Handsome! Mr. Isaiah. My…my…my…his smile! I could look at this man all day and not say a word. I was giggling and grinning from ear to ear like a teenaged girl.

Straight No Chaser: The Beginning

"Isaiah! Hey…you." I said shyly.

When he got to my car it was a little awkward. Should we hug? Handshake? Kiss on the cheek? Nothing? So, we opted to talk. No touching.

"I thought this was your car when I pulled up and to my surprise, I saw you walking out of Black Bean. Do you come here often?" he asked.

"Well, yeah maybe 3 times a week." I replied. I had to pick up some things for a meeting I'm running late for." I said as I looked at my watch.

At that moment my phone rang, when I looked down I saw it was Sarah, so I answered.

"Okay, great because as you see, I'm running late. Okay, well, I will see you guys and I still got the coffee and pastries," I told her.

We ended the call and I had a look of relief on my face.

"Whew good thing the meeting was postponed. The meeting Gods were looking out for me today," as we both laughed.

"I just wanted to say it was great meeting you the other day. And after you left I kicked myself for not asking for your number," he said smiling.

On the inside I was doing the running man and jumping up and down.

"Wow, really? I'm flattered," I said smiling.

"Yes, I would love to get to know you better," he said.

I wanted to rattle off my number to him but I didn't want to appear to be too pressed.

"Okay, I don't see anything wrong with that. You don't seem to be crazy," I said jokingly.

He laughed, "Are you sure, you sound a little hesitant there."

"Yes, a little, I can't lie. I'm always hesitant when giving out my number," I shyly said.

"It's no pressure, I understand totally, you don't know me from Adam; yeah I understand," he said.

"I tell you what, I'll give you *my* number and when you're ready, give me a call?"

I agreed and he gave me his business card.

We parted ways and I headed to work with a permanent smile on my face.

After we finally had our meeting that afternoon, I rushed back to my office to call Amy to let her know about Jake's phone call.

I sent her a text first before calling.

Hey girl, are you super busy? Jake called.

After 30 seconds my phone went off.

WHAT!? Call me!

Straight No Chaser: The Beginning

I picked up the phone and, after dialing, the phone hardly rang once. I laughed because she didn't even say 'hello' when she answered.

"Okay, start talking, what did he want?" she asked.

"Okay, after I got in the other night, I decided to check my voicemail on my house phone," I said.

"But you hardly use your house phone," she interrupted.

"Right. I hadn't checked it in weeks, so I decided to check it that night," I replied. To get to the point, he says that I had been on his mind a lot and asked if I would call him."

"Call him? Yeah whatever. Wait, you didn't call him did you?" she asked.

I took a deep a breath and said, "NOPE, at least not yet. Not too sure if I want to right now."

"Girl, don't call him. That girl he left you for is probably not all he thought she was cracked up to be. This is crazy," she said.

"Yeah, that's what I know, crazy indeed," I said.

"Well, if you decide to call him don't call him back right away. Get your mind together before you talk to him," she advised.

"That's the plan. I'm not ready to talk to him yet. I do miss him, it was good hearing his voice, if only for 30 seconds," I reflected.

I almost forgot to tell her about Mr. Handsome.

"Oh yeah, the other day after brunch and shopping, I stopped by my bakery for cheesecake. I saw this guy sitting in there chillin' out, right? Fine, girl! Well, he came to introduce himself and we parted ways. Fast forward to this morning, I saw him again at Black Bean; he saw me across the parking lot when I was trying to leave. Girl, he asked for my number!" I belted out, talking fast.

Amy interrupted, "Let me guess, you gave him the shy role like you didn't really want his number, right?" she said sarcastically.

I laughed, "Shut up and let me tell my story, please, ma'am, thank you."

She laughed and said, "Mmmm-hmmm, go ahead."

"I mean, really, I didn't want to come off as being too pressed. But he gave me his business card and now the ball's in my court to call him," I said.

"Hey, well, good for you for stepping out of your box, I'm proud of you," Amy said. "Well, when you call him, just play it cool and don't move too fast."

"Right, I'm definitely not in a rush for anything," I assured her.

We hung up the phone and I got busy on the mountain of work I needed to get done before leaving work. I knew I was going to be leaving work late, especially since I had a deadline coming up soon.

Straight No Chaser: The Beginning

As I guessed, I didn't leave work until after 7 PM. Since I left so late and the day left me stressed, I needed to go for a run. As I got into my car, I sat there for a minute to de-stress before starting the car. I sat in the quiet for what seemed to be an hour with my eyes closed and my head laid on the head rest, until my quietness was broken by a knock on the window.

I jumped and gasped, of course. As I looked up, I saw it was my boss.

"Oh, I'm sorry I didn't mean to startle you," he said as I was rolling down my window.

"Don't worry about it, George. I thought you had left for the day already," I inquired.

"Oh no, I'm doing the same as you, working on this big account. Are you running into any problems?" he asked.

Now the last thing I wanted to do was talk about work after I had left the building.

"No problems, I'm just trying to make sure all the numbers make sense," I said.

"Yeah, that's the tedious part, but I have faith in you. Well, you get home safely," he said while walking to his car. He stopped and turned around and said, "Xenia, the management team has been noticing your hard work, especially on this project. Keep up the good work, a promotion may be in the near future."

"Really, I didn't know you were looking to promote," I said excitedly.

"Well, we weren't, but, like I said, Management has been noticing your work, even before you were assigned this project," he said.

"Wow, George, that's awesome! Please don't worry, I will go above and beyond, as always, on this project," I assured him.

I watched as he walked away to his car.

Wow! Being on the Management team with George would be amazing—the perks, the expense account.

I was on cloud nine. That bit of news put me in a good place. I started the car and darted out of the parking lot. I was feeling adventurous, so the first stop light I got to, I picked up my phone and called Mr. Handsome. Great, his voicemail picked up. I was kind of glad because I was nervous about calling him.

"Hi, Mister! This is Zen. Surprise!! I don't think you thought I'd call this soon and I have to admit I didn't either. You now have my number, give me a call back."

I hung up the phone and let out a sigh of relief and said out loud, "Okay, Zen, you did it. Hi-five, girl!"

After getting home I started to cook dinner. I had been spending way too much going out every night. Since it was late, I kept it simple and made *shrimp alfredo*. While the food was simmering, I hopped in the shower to unwind and get the "day" off of me.

I fixed my plate and a glass of wine and watched TV. I tried to watch one of the news stations but after five minutes of bad news, I changed the channel. Then, I heard my phone ring; I had to look for it because I couldn't remember where I placed it after coming home. I finally found it before whomever went to voicemail.

"Hello?" I said out of breath.

A man's voice answered back, "Well, hello there. Ms. Xenia, how are you?"

"I'm okay, who's this?" I asked.

"You don't know who this is? Awe, man I'm hurt," he joked.

"I'm sorry, who's this?" I asked again. Now, I was laughing.

"This is Isaiah," he finally said.

Oh, my Lord, this man sounds even better over the phone.

"Oh, well, hello sir, how are YOU?" I asked.

"I'm doing okay, better now that I hear your voice," he slyly said.

"Okay, Isaiah, one thing about me. I cannot take the lines that men spit out. Just talk to me, no need for anything extra," I said, shaking my head.

Straight No Chaser: The Beginning

"Oh no, no games here. I'm sincere in all things but I understand, and no worries," he said apologetically.

We both laughed until there was a moment of silence.

Then I spoke up, "So, how was your day after seeing you at Black Bean?"

"My day was hectic and flew by, thank God. How was yours?" he asked.

"Oh my God, the same. I'm working on a big project at work and the deadline is nearing, so, of course, everything is uber-chaotic right now. So what kind of work do you do," I asked.

"Well, I'm a lawyer. I mainly deal with mergers. Right now, my firm is working on one of the biggest mergers by far for the year," he said.

"Sounds exhausting," I replied.

"Yep, pretty much. Long days, long nights. I'm actually taking a break now to call you back. So, what have you been up to this evening?" he asked.

"Well, I just got home not too long ago from work myself. I made dinner and now I'm relaxing with a glass of wine," I replied.

"Sounds very relaxing. So, you cook?" he asked sounding surprised.

Straight No Chaser: The Beginning

I laughed and said, "I'm not a gourmet chef, but, yes, I do cook. Although tonight's the first night I've cooked in a while. You sound surprised at the fact that I cook," I said.

"Yes, most women I know don't really cook. Why don't you cook a lot?" he asked.

"It's just me and I've never gotten it down, how to cook for one person. I don't really do leftovers after one day. So, I started to opt out of cooking and into picking up something on my way home."

"That's cool, I understand that. I love it when a woman cooks." he said.

Here we go.

"Really, you like that? Well, just FYI, I only cook for my man," I said.

He lets out a laugh, "I wasn't trying to imply…"

I interrupted him mid-sentence laughing, "Yeah, yeah, yeah sure."

"No seriously, I wasn't trying to imply anything, but it's nice to know you're not a stranger to the kitchen." he said.

"Nope, not at all," I assured him. So what's your story Isaiah? I know you're a lawyer, but, are you dating—girlfriend, wife?"

I could hear him chuckle. "Wow, right out of the gate huh? Straight, no chaser?"

"Yes, sir. I don't believe in having my time wasted. I try to avoid it at all costs" I said.

I paused, waiting for him to give me an answer. All while praying he was not attached to anyone. But, *his* pause made *me* pause!

"Well, no, I don't have a girlfriend. Man. Can you hold on for a sec, it's my other line," he asked.

He placed me on hold and I took another bite of food and sip of wine. I hated being placed on hold, and just as I was about to hang up, he appeared back on the line.

"Hey, still there?" he asked.

"Almost wasn't! I was just about to hang up," I laughed.

"Oh, really?" he sounded surprised.

"Yep, I don't like to be put on hold for a certain amount of time," I told him.

"Okay, okay. Well, I apologize." "So where were we? Are *you* attached to anyone?" he inquired.

Mr. Handsome think he's slick. He didn't finish answering my question, but I'll come back to it.

"Me, no, I'm not attached. If I were, we wouldn't be on the phone right now," I said.

"Really?" he asked.

"Yes, really. I don't do the double, triple time with people. I don't have the energy for it," I said.

"To do what?" he asked.

"Cheat or spread myself thin," I replied.

"I hear you, yeah, I understand," he said.

This conversation was going downhill fast. Red flags everywhere!

I had to come up with an excuse to get off the phone because now I wasn't comfortable talking to him anymore, especially since he was avoiding my question about his relationship status.

"Oh, my gosh, I have to call you back, I completely forgot to call my mom before it got too late," I said.

"Oh…yeah. Maybe we can link up and get coffee or something?" he asked.

"Ok let me look at my schedule and I'll let you know," I said quickly, hanging up the phone.

How stupid does he think I am?

Chapter 9

I was sitting at my desk when my assistant came in with a huge smile on her face. I looked up perplexed.

"What's wrong with you?" I asked.

"Oh, my goodness, I don't know what you're doing but, once again, you have a bouquet of the most gorgeous flowers!" she exclaimed.

I immediately rolled my eyes and shook my head because I thought they were from Jake.

"Hold on. I'll bring them in," she said.

"Oh my, they are definitely beautiful," I admitted, surprisingly.

This was definitely not Jake's style.

"You can sit them down over there?" I instructed.

Sarah disappeared behind the door.

I walked over to this gorgeous display and read the card.

I've waited long enough, have coffee with me?

Isaiah

How in the world did he know where I worked? I didn't recall telling him where I worked during our brief conversations. Oh, Lord! He's a stalker.

Straight No Chaser: The Beginning

A few weeks had since passed by and I hadn't had the opportunity to speak to him again, mainly due to my deadline at work. I sat at my desk staring at the arrangement contemplating calling him. I decided not to call at that moment and got back to work.

I looked at the time and realized I hadn't eaten lunch. Who does that? So, I packed up my laptop and darted out of the office for a working lunch.

I settled into the spot at the table and ordered my lunch. I was so engrossed in my work I didn't hear the waiter come to the table with my food, I'm sure he called my name a few times before I looked up from my laptop.

"Oh, my goodness! I'm so sorry,"

I took a small break to eat a little, then back to work I went. That's when I felt a tap on my shoulder, which startled me as I looked up. It was Mr. Handsome himself. He smiled. I smiled.

I sat back in my chair and just looked at him.

"Sir, are you stalking me?" I smirked.

"Depends on your definition of *stalk*," he said jokingly.

I laughed, "Thank you for the flowers. But, how'd you know where I worked because I don't recall telling you that information."

He smiled, "Xenia, I have my ways of finding out information. But don't worry, little lady. I'll never use anything against you."

Straight No Chaser: The Beginning

"Against me? Oh Lord, you are stalker!" I laughed.

"I've been waiting on you to call for our coffee date," he said.

"Yeah, about that, I'm still working on this project and I have to give my boss an update later today," I said, apologetically.

"Ok, well, I'll let you get back to your work. I was on my way out and saw you sitting here," he explained. Xenia, I do want to get to know you better, if you allow me."

I looked at him and I felt myself soften a bit. I took a deep breath.

"I'd like that Isaiah. I'll give you a call when things settle on my end," I told him.

"Alright, I'll hold you to that," he said. By the way, you look very nice today," he said while walking away.

He left me there smiling from ear to ear. Dog gone you, Isaiah! Now, I have to refocus.

I finished up my lunch and rushed back to the office to print off my presentation for my boss. If I do say so myself, I dazzled. I had to pat myself on the back on this one. This had to be some of my best work. I was sure to be promoted by the Management team. After the team update with my boss, I couldn't help but be all smiles. As I was on my way home, I just had to celebrate…but *how* was the question.

Straight No Chaser: The Beginning

As I pulled into my driveway, I realized it was the first time I had arrived home with the sun still out. So, I went for a run.

Running always put me in a better place. Although I had a great day at work, it was still stressful and I needed to distress.

My five-mile run rejuvenated my body and definitely my mind. As I was stretching in my driveway, a car pulled in. My senses went on high alert because I hadn't planned on anyone coming by tonight and I didn't recognize the car. I continued stretching and watched my surroundings in case I needed to make another run for it.

The car door opened and, to my surprise, it was Amy.

"Wait. A new car!? Well, aren't we fancy?" I said looking through the car.

"Yes, like it?" she asked.

"The job is treating us well I see!" I told her.

"Yes, the promotion I was up for came through and the money hit my account a few weeks ago," she said.

"This is so nice girl! You have a big girl car now," we both laughed.

I invited her inside after a tour of the car. As we walked into the house we headed to the kitchen and I offered her a glass of wine. She passed so I grabbed us both bottles of water from the fridge.

Straight No Chaser: The Beginning

"So how many miles did you run today?" she asked.

"Five and my feet are killing me. It must be time for new running shoes." I told her. Today was the first day I've run in a couple of weeks." I said.

"Well it's good to see you back at it since I know how much you love it." she said. Have you signed up for any races," she asked.

"I signed up for one, but my work load has been so crazy that I'm scared I won't have time to fit in the training," I explained.

"Speaking of work and since we haven't chatted in forever, I am up for a promotion as well! Depending on how this project goes that my team is working on, I could be promoted to the Management team. If that happens, girl the perks that will come with it, make me do my happy dance!" I exclaimed.

Amy's eyes lit up and she said, "Oh my God, that's great! I know you weren't really looking for the Management role, but this is great news. Well, no wonder it's been tough getting up with you," she said.

"And let me fill you in on my little social life. I hadn't heard from Jake since he sent me flowers. But I'm sure he'll call me again since I'm talking about him. And I met this guy, Mr. Handsome, and he's been trying to get me to go out for coffee with him. And he sent me *those* flowers," I said, pointing into the living room.

Straight No Chaser: The Beginning

Amy turned around and peered into the living room and said, "Oh my, those are beautiful! What did he do, buy up all the flowers in the shop?" she said laughing.

We both laughed and I said, "Well you know those are my favorite. And I didn't tell him they were my favorite."

"Wow!" Amy said eagerly.

"Yeah, but I don't know about him, Amy. I asked him the other day about his relationship status and somehow he avoided the question. After I saw how he avoided the question, I just got off the phone with him."

"We don't have time for that. If you see this red flag, proceed with caution," Amy advised.

"Yeah, but he's *so* fine!" I said. But yes, red flag indeed. That's why it has taken me so long to respond to his date proposal."

"Understood. Well, girl let me get out of here so I can get back home." Amy said as she looked at her watch.

"Oh, alright," I said.

I forgot how much I missed my girl and didn't want her to leave.

"Love the car and congrats again on the promotion!" I told her.

"Thanks girl," she said. Good luck on your promotion and, remember, take it slow with Mr. Handsome," she said as she pointed at me.

"Yes ma'am." I replied throwing my hands up as if I were surrendering.

I walked back into the kitchen to figure out what was for dinner. I should have been cooking while I was talking to Amy, but I wanted to give her all of my attention. I took out a frozen dinner and heated it up and relaxed in front of the TV, until I drifted off to sleep.

I must have been tired because it was midnight when I finally woke up and realized not only was I still on the couch, but I was still in my running clothes. Gross! I pulled myself together, cleaned up my empty carton of food, took a shower and hit the sack.

Chapter 10

I was on my way to work and my phone began to ring. Since I was driving I hit the phone button on my steering wheel.

"Hello?" I asked.

"Wow, you're a hard lady to get in touch with," the voice answered.

There was dead air for what seemed like an hour.

"Ummm, hi…Jake? Good morning, how are you?" I asked.

I now *hate* I answered the phone.

"I'm great, sweetheart, how are you?" he asked.

"Please, don't call me that and I'm wonderful. How can I help you today?" I asked.

"Why so formal?" Jake replied.

"Sorry. I'm already in work mode, trying to put out fires," I said.

"Oh, okay, well I won't keep you long," he said.

I interrupted, "I've been meaning to return your call, but I have this big project at work I've been working on. Thanks for the flowers."

I knew I was lying but it wasn't totally a lie, I was working on a project.

"Cool. I know the first call after a break up can be awkward. It took me two weeks to actually pick up the phone. I just wanted…" he said and paused.

"Hello? Jake you still there," I asked.

"Yes, I'm still here, I'm sorry, guess this is the awkward part," he said.

"The awkward part? This entire call is awkward," I said as I gave a half laugh.

Then he blurted out, "I miss you! There I said it. I miss you, Zen. I can't stop thinking about you no matter how hard I try."

I can't lie, hearing him say that made me feel good, but at the same time ticked me off.

"I'm sorry, did you say you missed me?" I asked him.

"Yeah." he responded.

I paused. Then I let out a deep sigh.

"Wow, Jake, I don't know what to say," I said.

"Can we meet for dinner later this week?" he asked.

I couldn't believe what I was hearing. This guy. Is this really how my morning was starting?

"Look Jake, I…" I said, as I paused.

"You don't have to answer now. Think about it and let me know," he said.

"Jake, I'm pulling into work. I have to call you back." I disconnected the call before either of us could say goodbye.

I sat in the car and choked back tears. I couldn't believe this. Where was all of this emotion coming from? Why today? Ugh, I couldn't deal.

I sat in the car a few minutes extra to get myself together and then I headed into work. I couldn't believe it but, it took me half of my work day to get into a groove and *almost* forget that phone call.

I needed an escape. So, I picked up my phone.

"Hey, Isaiah, this is Xenia, how are you?" I asked

"Whoa, is it going to snow today?" he said jokingly.

"I know right! Listen, I was wondering if you weren't busy if you'd like to meet for lunch today," I asked.

Why was I doing this now? Maybe it wasn't the smartest thing, but I needed a distraction.

"Well, for you, I'll meet you. When are you leaving?" he asked.

"I'm starving, so now," I said laughing.

We decided to meet at a new restaurant in town. I cleaned up my desk a little and headed out. I was so nervous my palms were sweating.

I walked into the restaurant and saw he beat me there. When he saw me he waved for me to come over to the table. The table was a little secluded which made me more nervous.

As I got closer to the table he stood to greet me and gave me a hug when I reached the table. He even pulled my seat out for me. Okay, Mr. Handsome, I see you! Gentlemen were my weakness. He sat across from me and smiled.

"Finally, I get some of your time!" he said.

"Yeah, I figured why not today."

I dare not tell him the *real* reason.

The waiter took our orders and we began to have the awkward first-time talks.

"So, now that you have my attention, finish telling me about yourself, Isaiah."

"Well you know I'm a lawyer. I'm from a small town in North Carolina. I'm 38 years old and I have two kids; twins and they are in Washington," he said.

"Really, two kids? So, what's your relationship like with their mom or moms?" I asked.

"One mom, and our relationship is okay, we keep the kids first, but you know we have our days," he said.

"How'd you get here? I know you must miss your kids a lot," I said.

"I do miss them, but they're almost old enough for either a train or plane ride out to see me. I think they may come to visit for part of the summer. But, we talk on the phone & Skype a lot," he said.

"Well, it sounds like you have a good relationship with them. Which is good," I said.

"I'm here because of the job. I never really wanted to move, but this was truly an offer I couldn't refuse," he said.

"Gotcha. So, what about the relationship with your kids' mom? I know you said you keep the kids first. But are you two still together, married, still sleeping with each other?" I asked.

I couldn't let this question go unanswered again.

"Wow, straight, no chaser huh?" he asked.

"Yep, that's me! These are things I need and like to know regardless of where 'this' goes," I said.

"Understood," he said.

The waiter brought out our food, but I was not going to let him evade this question again. I stared at him until he realized I was not about to let the question slide.

"Oh, your question. I'm separated," he divulged, reluctantly.

A piece of me died a little. Separated? Gosh, well, I'll have to readjust.

"How long have you been separated?" I asked.

"Almost six months," he replied.

"Okay, is that the other reason you moved?" I asked.

"Yeah, we both needed to move forward with our lives and the job came at, I guess, the right time." he said.

Other than him telling me he was separated, the lunch was actually pretty good. Maybe that's a good thing. It'll keep me from potentially falling for him and from doing anything stupid.

When the check came, I reached for it. Since I asked him to lunch, I was expecting to take care of the check. When he saw I was reaching for it, he immediately snatched it out of my grasp.

"Um, excuse me, I asked you to lunch so, therefore, I'm paying," I said.

"Yeah right. If you're out with me, you don't have to worry about paying for anything. I don't care if you did ask me out," he said with a smirk.

I smirked and said, "Yes, sir, okay. In that case, thanks for lunch, Isaiah."

Isaiah walked me to my car, we engaged in a little small talk and we parted our ways back to work.

I got in the car to head back to work and picked up the phone.

I sent Amy a quick text.

finally went to lunch with Mr. Handsome. He's separated

Straight No Chaser: The Beginning

My phone's text notification went off and it was Amy's response.

*☺ *blank stare**

I laughed and shook my head.

Chapter 11

"**Xenia**, you've done a superb job on the acquisition and we wanted to be the first to congratulate you on being the newest member to the Management team," Gregory said.

I wanted to jump up and down but I contained myself. I had a permanent smile on my face, like the Cheshire Cat grin. That was me!

Being on the Management team wasn't even something I realized I wanted and needed until my boss told me I was being considered. The perks were great, but never mind that right now. Right now, I'm looking at the experience I'll gain being in this position. More responsibility and possible headache, yes…but, oh, so worth it in the end.

The first perk I got to take advantage of, taking off two days. But, before taking off for my long weekend, I was able to treat my team to lunch. Let's face it; I wouldn't have gotten to this place without those guys.

After taking the team to lunch, we all went home at 3 PM. As for me, I'd be off the remainder of the week! As I was driving home, I began to think about how grateful I was. I felt the tears form from my toenails and fill my eyes. They began to stream down my face. I wanted to call and share my awesome news with Amy but she wasn't available when I called. I just left a message letting her know the promotion was finalized.

The next person I called? Jake. I'm not sure why I called him, but I did. I knew I would regret it, but as the phone rang, I continued to listen to it ring hoping he wouldn't answer.

"Hello?" he said.

"Hey…Hi, Jake. How are you?" I stuttered.

"Well, Hey Zen. How are you? Is everything ok?" he asked.

"Yeah, everything's good." I laughed nervously. You were on my mind and I thought I'd call," I said.

"It's good to hear from you. What's going on with you today?" he asked.

"Well, today's been a great day. I got a promotion today, so I'm basking in my excitement!" I said.

"Congrats, Zen! I'm sure you're deserving. You must have made a great impression on your project, huh?" he asked.

"Yeah, I guess so."

"So what are you doing to celebrate?" he asked.

"I hadn't even thought about celebrating to be honest. I hadn't thought that far ahead. I don't know." I said baffled.

"Well, you have to celebrate. Let me take you to dinner," he offered.

"Dinner? Don't you have a girlfriend?" I asked.

"About that—no. We actually aren't together anymore," he confessed.

There was a brief pause as I gave my phone the side eye.

"Wow, really?" I asked. I sound underwhelmed.

"Yeah, so dinner? Tonight?" he asked.

There was another pause.

"Jake, I…" I said.

He cut me off mid-sentence, "I know I may not deserve dinner, but I'd love to see you."

Reluctantly I said, "Okay, sure, dinner tonight sounds…it sounds good."

"Great! Tonight it is. Should I pick you up?" he asked.

I quickly said, "No. Jake this is not a date. I'll meet you at 7:30 PM at that Italian place on Roneldo Drive."

"Okay, cool…" he paused. I will be there at 7:30PM."

As we got off the phone, I couldn't believe what I had just agreed to doing. Dinner with the guy that cheated on me and lied to me for months! I just called to share good news.

I blamed Amy for not answering her phone!

Oh my god! What did I just do!? He was right, he didn't deserve dinner or to even talk to me after what he did, but, hey, the dinner was going to be that…DINNER. Absolutely nothing more.

Straight No Chaser: The Beginning

I decided to workout at the gym since I had more than enough time today. I ran a few miles on the dreadmill and lifted some weights. I'd feel the weights tomorrow and possibly the next day as well.

After I worked out I sat in the sauna before heading home to get ready for this dinner thing I agreed to.

This was going to be tricky because when I go out with someone of the opposite sex, I go all out when it comes to my outfits. I didn't quite know how to dress for a 'I really don't want to be out with him, but I am because; well I don't know why I'm here' thing-a-ma-jiggy.' So, jeans and heels it was. I was still cute, but not quite what I would normally do.

I was running late leaving the house so, I ran out of the house, which proved to be tricky because of my workout earlier. I sent Jake a quick text letting him know I was running late and on the way. He was running late, too, so I felt a little better and slowed down to catch my breath.

Jake and I actually pulled into the parking lot at the same time, but I parked a few spaces down from him.

We walked in and the hostess gave us this ginormous smile.

"Welcome you two, how are you?" she asked.

"We're good," we said in unison.

"Right this way," she instructed.

As we were following her I noticed she was taking us to the dimly lit, somewhat secluded section of the restaurant.

"Ma'am, where are you taking us?" I asked.

"Oh, I thought you two would like it here," she responded.

"Oh, um, yeah we can sit towards the front in an area that's well lit, please," I told her.

"Yes ma'am, right this way," she said.

I know I put a wrench in her plan, but nope, not tonight. I have to keep my eye on him—no funny business.

"Okay, love birds, here we go," she said smiling as she sat the menus down on the table.

"Thank you," we said again in unison.

"Well, Ms. Zen, thanks again for meeting me tonight," Jake said.

"No problem J," I said.

"We're calling me J, again?" he asked while smiling.

I hadn't realized I had even called him that as I was looking over the menu. I looked up from the menu.

With one eyebrow raised I said, "Sorry, didn't mean for that to slip out, but somewhat of a habit, I guess."

"It's okay, Zen, kind of nice to hear you call me that," Jake said.

Straight No Chaser: The Beginning

I shook my head and continued to look at the menu. We placed our drink and food orders and then the awkward silence happened.

"Well, okay, let's break this awkwardness," he said.

I interrupted, "Yes, I agree, so, why'd you ask me to dinner? I'm very curious."

"Straight to it, huh?" he asked.

"Come on J, you know me. Straight, no chaser. Now answer my question. Please." as I cleared my throat.

"Okay, like I told you on the phone, I miss you and I wanted to see you. I thought it was a great idea, especially since you were promoted today."

Our drinks came at the right time. I ordered a shot of whiskey to sip but I downed it in 0.5 seconds...flat!

"So, you missed me? That's very interesting to me because a few months ago this wasn't your story. You couldn't wait to get away from me," I reminded him.

"You're right. Zen, I just want to apologize for lying to you," he said.

I was surprised to hear what I was hearing. What was he up to?

"J, why'd you and your girl break up?" I asked.

He looked away and said, "Honestly, she didn't trust me after we got together."

I laughed. Hysterically.

"Wait. So, let me get this straight. The person you cheated on me with couldn't trust you!? Whoa!" I said still laughing.

"Yeah, but I wasn't cheating or lying to her," he said.

"Karma." I said shaking my head.

Our food came to the table and looked amazing. The waiter refilled our waters and I ordered a whiskey sour this time.

"So you thought that asking me out and telling me this would do what?" I asked.

"I didn't think anything. I just wanted to see you. I told you, I missed you," he said.

"Ok J," I said. You know what, let's just enjoy this food and the night."

I didn't want to argue with him or eat dinner with all of this tension. I like food too much to disrespect it like that. We spent the rest of the meal talking about our jobs and my promotion. Surprisingly, it was a good night.

Jake walked me to my car after we finished up dinner.

"J, thank you for tonight, for dinner. I, surprisingly, had a pretty good time," I admitted.

"Yeah, Zen, I'm not so bad right?" he said laughing.

"You're alright."

I laughed.

There was another pause of awkward silence. Jake hugged me. Tight. And, man, did it feel good. I hadn't realized how long it had been since I had another body against mine. Not in a sexual way, just, affection.

I cleared my throat and pulled away from him.

"Sorry, I just..." he said.

"J, it's okay." I interrupted as he stared deep into my eyes. What? Why are you staring?"

"You're so beautiful," he said.

"Typical. J, let's not go there ok?" I said. "I did not agree to meet you tonight to try and rekindle anything and before you try kissing me, I'm saying good night."

I got in my car. Presumptuous, but I couldn't take any chances and I needed to get out of there. Besides, I think I wanted him to kiss me.

Chapter 12

My days off proved to be more than needed. I slept until 11 AM every day. The first day I did absolutely nothing, but clean my house. I didn't realize I had slacked this much on my domestic duties.

After I completed a deep cleansing of my house, I celebrated with a nice glass of Chatham Hill white wine on my couch in the quiet. Perfect day.

After keeping my cell phone off all day, I decided to reconnect with the real world. My notifications were going crazy; between the emails, voicemail and texts, I wanted to throw my phone through the window!

I was so engrossed on my catching up, when I realized, I hadn't eaten all day. This was starting to be a really bad habit. I decided to just stay in for the night and cook.

I had been dying to try this new recipe and why not try it out tonight? I went to the kitchen to see if I had all the ingredients. Just my luck, I had to go to the store. That meant putting on clothes and I had been in the house all day. Now, I had to decide if I really wanted to make this dish.

After debating with myself for about ten minutes, I decided to get up and make that store run anyway. I walked into the grocery store and walked the aisles in case I needed other items as well. This was awesome, because I hated grocery shopping. Since I was going to barricade myself in my house for the weekend, I decided to try some dessert recipes as well.

"Oh I could make banana pudding on Sunday, I haven't made that in a long time," I said out loud.

"I love your banana pudding," I heard a man's voice say.

I turned around quickly in case I needed to defend myself.

It was Jake.

"Hey J. You almost got hit sneaking up on me like that," I said with an eye roll.

"My bad. But I do love your banana pudding," he said.

"Thanks."

I turned to walk away.

Why did I do that? He thought it was an invite to follow me.

"It's like that Zen?" he asked looking sad.

"Don't look at me like that, J," I said.

He makes the cutest sad face that I could never resist.

"J, stop following me, please," I laughed.

"I know you couldn't hold it in much longer," he said laughing.

"Shut your face!" I said, still laughing.

"It's good to see you again, second day in a row. You know how that could be looked at right?" he said.

I interrupted him, "As nothing. We're just both here at the same time, sir, nothing more, nothing less."

"Awe, Zen, come on now. I'm just playing," he said.

"Mmmhmm," I said, as I gave him a side eye.

"Do I get an invite for dinner and dessert?" he finally asked.

"Man, you're bold," I said. Who are you here with anyway?" I asked.

"I came in for toilet paper and looked up and saw your beautiful face," he said.

"You're too kind. Please…STOP!" I said.

This going back and forth was working on my last nerve. I looked over and there he was, Mr. Handsome. Great I looked like crap! But, at least my hair was done.

We caught each other's eyes and he began to walk towards me.

"Zen…Zen! Are you listening to me?" Jake asked.

I had zoned out, watching Isaiah walk over.

"What? I'm sorry, what did you say?" I asked Jake.

"Nothing, I was messing with you," he said.

Straight No Chaser: The Beginning

Mr. Handsome had finally made it over to myself and Jake.

"Well, hello there, how are you?" I asked. I had the biggest smile on my face.

"I'm well, thank you for asking," he said.

Jake cleared his throat, which broke my trance.

"This is Jake, Jake this is Isaiah," I said as I introduced them.

Ugh, I wanted Jake to walk away but that was asking too much! They both shook hands. (Insert awkward silence.) I looked at Jake and gave him the 'please leave' look.

"Oh, Zen it was great seeing you again. Call me when you make the banana pudding. I'd love to come by for some." he said.

Jerk. I didn't answer. I just smiled and let out a deep sigh.

"I didn't interrupt anything, did I?" Isaiah asked.

"A welcomed interruption," I said laughing.

"So, we're making banana pudding?" he inquired.

Thanks Jake.

"Uh yeah, at some point this weekend," I said.

"Homemade or that instant pudding stuff?" he said as he turned up his nose.

Straight No Chaser: The Beginning

"Do you see any instant pudding in my cart," I replied laughing. I try to make everything from scratch, FYI."

"Okay, okay, I see you," he said flashing those pretty teeth of his. Good to know."

"Why good to know?" I asked.

"It's just good to know," he said.

"Anyway, how's your day been?" I asked.

"It's been good, busy, but good. I think we're close to wrapping up the merger and then I'll be able to breathe again," he said.

"Good for you," I said.

My phone began to ring, thank God. I remembered I still needed to cook.

"Hello?" I said. Hey girl! Yes. I'm at the store picking up things for dinner. Meet me at the house. Oh and what bottle of wine would you like? Okay, see ya in a few!" I said as I hung up the phone.

"I'm holding you up," he said, apologetically.

"It's okay, Jake was talking my head off earlier, so I can make a little time for you. But, I do have to get out of here now," I said.

"Yeah, I heard. No worries, give me a call later," he said. It was good seeing you." He began walking away.

"It was good seeing you, too," I replied walking away.

I wondered if he was watching me walk away this time. I wanted to look but didn't want to look stupid, again. So, I kept walking this time.

Amy was waiting on me when I got to my house.

I jumped out of the car, "Hey girl!" I exclaimed. Help me with these bags."

"Hey girl! Where have you been? I started to call the police," she said jokingly.

"Well, first, I got my promotion yesterday!" I exclaimed, doing my happy dance.

Amy screamed and danced with me for the entire neighborhood to see and hear.

"AND…I had dinner with J last night. Before you drop my groceries come in the house so I can tell you all about it, and stop looking at me like that," I demanded.

"Wait, what?" she asked, looking perplexed.

As we walked into the house I sat the keys on the table and locked the door behind us, and jetted to the kitchen.

"Ok, it's your fault; you didn't answer your phone!" I said jokingly. "Kidding!"

"I knowwwww…I missed your call, now I really hate I missed your call," she said.

"But, surprisingly, it went way better than I thought," I said.

Straight No Chaser: The Beginning

I started putting up the groceries and cooking us dinner.

"Okay, sooo…how'd you two get to dinner?" she asked as I poured our two glasses of wine.

"Ha! Well, after I couldn't get in touch with you to tell you my good news,…"

Amy interrupted me, "So, you *called* him!?"

"It wasn't like that. I didn't call with the intention of telling him. It just fell out of my mouth when he asked about work. Then he asked what I was doing to celebrate and, at the time, I wasn't doing anything, so he asked me to dinner and wouldn't take no for an answer." I explained all in one run-on sentence.

"I can't believe she had dinner with the enemy," Amy said shaking her head.

"He said he missed me. Don't look at me like that; I didn't fall for any of his shenanigans. He said he and that girl broke up, too. And get this—because she couldn't trust him. HA!" I said laughing.

"Ohhhhh, the side chick couldn't trust him, big surprise!" Amy joked.

"Right. That's what I told him. He walked me to my car and, girl, I forgot how long it had been since I had been hugged, because when he did, WOOO!! I thought he was going to try and kiss me, but I jumped in the car and left." I said, taking a sip of wine.

"Good for you!" Amy said.

Straight No Chaser: The Beginning

"And...," I said.

"Oh, gosh," Amy interrupted.

"This isn't crazy at all. Lunch with Mr. Handsome went okay. I told you he was separated, right?" I asked.

"Yeah," Amy said.

"He's been separated for about six months."

"Girl, he's still married and that's too soon in my opinion," Amy said.

"Yeah, I know and it sucks! And I saw him at the store a few minutes ago which means he may live on this side of town," I told her.

Amy laughed.

"It's not funny!" I said.

Dinner was finally done and we sat at the table and laughed and talked some more.

"Okay, so, enough about me. What's going on with you?" I asked Amy, intrigued. She had been getting closer with her new man.

"Not much, I'm finally happy. Everything seems to be falling into place or has fallen into place. Every day isn't a bed of roses, but I'm happy," she said with the biggest smile.

I sat and I took in everything she was saying. Amy was a little hard to please sometimes so when she was telling me all was well, I knew she wasn't lying. I was excited for her and her future. She was beyond deserving of her happiness.

"Awe, Boo, I'm so happy for you. A little envious, but I'm sooo happy for you," I told her.

She looked at me and we both had tears in our eyes. Then we burst out laughing at each other because we were the biggest saps in the world.

"Girl, your happiness is on the way," she assured me.

"Yeah, I know, it's on the way, everything is going well in my life. I'm just trying to get a handle on this love life of mine," I told her. "But, I'm trying not to worry about that. I'm trying to get past J and then I'll be good."

"Girl, you've got this, it takes time, you know that," Amy said.

"Yeah, I just wish he wasn't trying to get back in my good graces or whatever you want to call it," I said as I rolled my eyes.

"Agreed." Amy said astutely while holding up her wine glass.

"Let us pray," I said.

Amy looked at me like I was crazy.

"Lord, please don't let me fall for this fool, again, after what he did to me. Block the fools Lord, block the FOOLS! Amen," I said.

Amy burst out laughing.

"Yes Lord, block the fools!" she mimicked me while taking a sip of wine.

We both laughed.

"Man, I have some crazy friends," Amy said.

"Oh…and you support my crazy. Sometimes," I responded.

I laughed and took our empty plates to the kitchen counter for more food and discovered we had eaten everything I cooked.

"Hey, since you're up, I want more pasta ma'am," Amy said.

I laughed, "We ate it all. I wanted more, too."

"Oh, well, suppose I didn't need any more, huh?" Amy said.

"I think I'm making a chocolate pie tomorrow, if you want to stop by. I know for sure I'm making a banana pudding Sunday," I said.

The one thing I loved about Amy was she loved to eat just as much as I did. So she was always up to trying new dishes or restaurants with me.

"Man, I didn't realize it was this late," Amy said.

I was cleaning up the kitchen and putting the remainder of the dishes in the dishwasher.

"What time is it?" I asked.

"It's almost 11 PM!" Amy said.

"I stopped keeping track of the time since I don't have to be back to work until Monday morning," I said with a smirk.

"Yeah, yeah, yeah. Well, you let me know if you make that chocolate pie. If not, I'll see you Sunday for my banana pudding girl," she said.

I walked her to the door and watched her until she pulled out of the driveway. I walked back into the kitchen to sweep up, poured another glass of wine and watched TV.

While Amy was with me, I totally forgot about my phone. I picked it up and saw I had text messages from J and Mr. Handsome. I was on such a high, I didn't bother reading either of their messages. I continued to watch TV for the rest of the night.

Chapter 13

As my extended staycation was coming to an end, I sat in bed on this wonderful beautiful Sunday morning and took everything in. I got up and fixed my morning coffee. While my coffee was brewing, I decided to attend the early service at my church. I got dressed, had a few more cups of coffee and off I went.

Church was just what I needed. I hadn't been in what felt like forever. I arrived just in time. My Pastor had just gotten up to the pulpit so I grabbed a seat on the last pew.

After church I went to speak to the parentals. You would've thought I had just gotten back from the war the way my mom acted.

"Mom, I know I haven't been here in a while, but you're acting like you haven't seen me in forever," I said.

"Well, glad to see you here this morning, baby," she said.

"Hey daddy." I said as I hugged him.

"Hey, surprised to see you at the early service," he said.

When I did come to church I never came to the early service, the later the service was better for me.

"Yeah, I was up early today so I decided to go ahead and get my day started," I told him.

"Well, it's good to see you," he assured me.

Straight No Chaser: The Beginning

My parents had a meeting after service so we parted ways. As I was walking out of the church I stopped to talk to various people I hadn't seen in forever. When I finally got outside to get to my car, I looked over and who do I see? Mr. Handsome. He saw me and came over to my car.

I shake my head at him and asked, "You are stalking me?" We both laughed.

"No ma'am, I've been visiting here the past month," he said.

"Oh, wow, really?"

"Yep. So far I love it!" he said.

"That's great!"

"What's wrong?" he asked.

"Not a thing."

"Is this your first time here?" he asked.

I smirked and said, "Nope. I actually grew up in this church."

His eyes lit up.

"Isn't that something? Ms. Zen, I think the stars are lining up," he said.

"Lining up for what?" I asked.

Isaiah laughed, "Xenia, Xenia. So how'd dinner go with your friend the other night?"

As I was scanning the parking lot, I spotted my parents coming out of the church. My mom looked and saw me talking to Mr. Handsome.

Oh, great, I could hear our conversation later. I looked back at him quickly.

"Dinner, oh, we had fun catching up. Listen give me a call later? I forgot I had to be somewhere in 45 minutes," I said frantically.

I didn't even stick around to see what his response was, I jumped in my car and left.

As soon as I got onto the road my phone rings. I didn't bother looking to see who it was.

"Hey ma," I said.

"Nope, not mama..." the male voice said. It was Isaiah.

"You okay? You sped away so fast. I wanted to invite you to brunch."

"Isaiah. Sorry for being rude, I just...I saw my parents and, since my mom tries to sell me off to the highest bidder, I didn't want her interrogating either of us," I admitted.

"I understand. My mom can be like that too," he laughed.

"She's going to interrogate me anyway the next time she talks to me. But no need subjecting you to that today."

I was hoping Mr. Handsome was going to "forget" about brunch, since we were talking about my mother.

"So, about brunch today?" he asked again.

"Isaiah, I have to be completely honest with you. I know you said you're separated but you're still married AND you've only been separated a short time. I am not going to risk letting my guard down to get hurt. I can't do it," I said.

After telling him that I felt some relief and some of the weight I was carrying had definitely lifted off my shoulders.

There was silence.

"Is there anything wrong with us being friends?" he asked.

Typical response.

"Friends? Sure, I'd like that."

In the back of my mind I was thinking I needed to be extra careful with this one. It felt like he had something up his sleeve.

"Well, good. So, what's wrong with two friends getting something to eat?" he asked.

I knew that was going to be his next line. But I had to give it to him, he was persistent.

I shook my head, smirked and let out a sigh.

"Isaiah, I can't today," I told him.

I honestly couldn't make it to brunch with him or anyone else for that matter.

Straight No Chaser: The Beginning

"Alright, Ms. Xenia, you're missing out on some great company," he said.

He sounded disappointed.

"I know exactly what I'm missing out on," I said.

We both laughed.

"Oh yeah, that's right you're making that banana pudding today, right?" he asked.

I laughed again, "Yep, sure am. You aren't going to let up are you?"

"Nope," he simply said.

"Maybe we could meet for lunch next week," I offered.

"You're killing me, Xenia," he said.

I was trying my best to stay away from Mr. Handsome. I know my weaknesses when it comes to men and he was everyone of them. Smile. Toned build. Ambitious. Intelligent. Sense of humor. Yeah, I needed to continue being by myself for a while. If that meant blowing him off, then so be it.

"Awe, I'm sorry," I said. I turned into the grocery store parking lot. I was glad I didn't have to shop for food. All I needed was champagne and juice then off to my house for a relaxing day.

"Okay, Isaiah, I've reached my destination. So, I'll hit you back later," I told him.

Straight No Chaser: The Beginning

I ran into the grocery store, picked up what I needed and rushed home to get everything started.

After getting home, I decided to go for a quick run before I started my mimosas and dinner. I changed into my running tights. I put my roast in the crock pot before leaving out so that would be one less thing I'd have to worry about when returning.

While I was running, I thought about how blessed I was to live the life I was living. Then Isaiah's face flashed in my head. Oh my gosh!! NO, NO, NO! This can't be happening. I stopped running to get myself together. I found a bench to stretch my legs before I hit the pavement again. Running was supposed to take the edge off. It wasn't; not with him flashing in my head.

I started running again and headed back home. Needless to say, I was exhausted after running five miles. I stretched in my drive way before going back into the house. When I walked back into the house, the aroma of the roast was already creeping through every nook and cranny. I couldn't wait to eat later. I walked into the kitchen to get a better smell of dinner and a bottle of water.

I cleaned myself up and got back in the kitchen to finish up dinner. I threw some baby carrots in with the roast and peeled the potatoes to boil for my famous garlic mashed potatoes. I decided to sauté my asparagus right before serving dinner, so I put those to the side. After all of that was done, I started the banana pudding. I had to be careful not to make too much especially since it's only me that lives in the house. I couldn't eat too much. I was working way too hard to maintain the weight I lost.

Everything was done and now I could rest up a bit. I decided to call my parents to invite them for dinner and I also called to remind Amy as well.

Now, it was time for mimosas. Then I realized I did it again. Forgot to eat! Who does that!? I fixed eggs and toast and it was divine; I was famished. I sat in front of the TV and caught up on my movies I'd missed during the week.

After three mimosas I decided to slow down, as I drifted off to sleep.

I woke up to my phone ringing. I looked at my phone and saw it was Jake. I let him go to voicemail. I was not up to being on my defenses with him this afternoon.

"God what does he want?" I exclaimed out loud.

I cleaned up my plate from my eggs and went into the kitchen to check on things. The roast still had another hour or so and I snuck a taste of the mashed potatoes and almost slapped myself, they were so good!

When everyone arrived for dinner, I offered them something to drink. Amy came in and fixed herself a mimosa. I braced myself for the 'who was that man you were talking to after church' conversation. But, thank God, mom never brought it up and neither did I.

I could not have asked for a more complete day before going back to work.

Chapter 14

"So Xenia, where's Jake been?" mom asked.

Oh the dreaded conversation was going to happen whether I liked it or not. I avoided it for good reason.

"Well...Hello, mom, how are you?" I replied.

"Mmmhmm, I'm fine. Now answer the question. I have been more than patient. I've noticed he hasn't been around and I got real suspicious when I saw you talking to that young man after church the other Sunday. Yes ma'am, I saw you dart away from him when you saw me coming out of church. Now spill it," she demanded.

Well, there it was, the other shoe finally dropped. Since I didn't prepare for this moment, there was a long pause of silence. I hate when she catches me off guard.

"Yes mom, we broke up months ago," I said.

"I figured that when he wasn't at Sunday dinner. What happened, child? You know what I'm asking, stop playing dumb," she said.

"Mom, we just didn't work out, now please leave it alone," I begged. I have a big day today at work and I don't want this on my mind," I told her.

"You shouldn't go through stuff alone, child."

"Ma, I'm not going through anything alone. It's just a break up and yes, I was hurt when it happened, but I'm getting

Straight No Chaser: The Beginning

better every day. I'm dealing the best way I know how," I assured her.

"Well that man you were talking to has been coming to the church regularly, maybe you should go out with him," she said.

Little did she know.

"Ok, Ma. Ma. I have to go now. I just pulled into the parking lot at work. I love you," I said as I hung up the phone.

That lady doesn't let up. If I know my mom, she's going to find out all she can about Mr. Handsome to fix us up. Oh my goodness. Oh well, can't do anything about it now.

As I was walking into work, my phone rang again and I just knew it was my mom. I looked down and saw that it was Mr. Handsome. I had been avoiding his calls for a couple of weeks now. I was not trying to get involved with this married man; separated or not. I am entirely too vulnerable to be around this fine man.

I walked into work and my assistant almost tackled me when she saw me coming. I could see how my morning and possibly entire day was going to go by her actions. Sarah gave me my messages, which were more than usual. This many calls since 8 AM!? I was overwhelmed already.

Sarah buzzed into my office and said, "Xenia, you have a phone call from an Isaiah? He said it was very important."

I rolled my eyes and let out a deep sigh.

"Sarah, please let him know I'm in a meeting and take a message," I told her.

"Will do." she said.

Not only was I avoiding his phone calls, but I was up to my eyeballs working on my first project as a Manager—a major acquisition and I did not have time to entertain him or anything he had to say.

I knew how persistent Isaiah was so I was just waiting for Sarah to reappear.

3...2...,"Xenia, he sounded...what's the word...FINE!" Sarah exclaimed as she burst back into my office.

Sarah had this knack of bursting into my office after 'questionable' phone calls she figured I was avoiding. Sarah was nosey, but she was also a great assistant and if I didn't divulge information she knew not to cross the line or continue to push the envelope.

I laughed, "Sarah leave it alone, please."

"Seriously, he sounded a little pressed to talk to you. So how long have you been avoiding his calls?" she asked as she sat down in the chair in front of my desk.

I looked up from my work and by my facial expression she knew she needed to get back to the work on her desk before she was handed a pink slip. (Yeah right, I would never get rid of her, she was a God-send.)

Straight No Chaser: The Beginning

Sarah left my office shaking her head, but I knew she was going to try to see who Isaiah really was later when I wasn't as stressed. But until then, back to work I went.

I decided to take a break and to take a stroll around the office; to show my face and to talk to the employees. With my being in the new Manager on the block, I felt the need to make myself more noticeable and especially more approachable. After I spoke to a few employees, I couldn't help but feel better about being a Manager. I knew every day would not be a bed of roses, but today was a good day.

As I was walking back to my office, I noticed a few of the Managers speaking with Sarah.

"Well, hello, everyone," I said cheerfully.

"Hello, Xenia," they said in unison. We were just stopping by to check in and to see how the project was going," George asked.

I motioned for them to come into the office.

"The project is going well so far. I thought I hit a road block, but I figured it out thank goodness!" I said.

"Good, that's what we like to hear." Henry said. Just to let you know next week we'll bring in the lawyers as well to work with you on this acquisition. We'll keep you posted on when that will be."

"Ok that sounds great," I said.

"You'll be working very closely with the legal team from this point forward as well," Henry said.

Straight No Chaser: The Beginning

"Ok, that shouldn't be a problem. And don't worry I know this acquisition is very important and know what it will mean to the company," I assured them.

After they left my office, I felt even better because, although still new to the team, they weren't micromanaging me.

I stepped over to the window in my office to just take in the scenery. This was a beautiful skyline and I couldn't wait to get out in the weather later for a run.

Sarah came in and handed me a report and gave me the messages from earlier.

"That Isaiah called again. All jokes aside, it sounded a little urgent," Sarah said.

I looked at her as she walked back out to her desk. I thought to myself, what could he possibly have to say to me that's so important?

Looking back at my view, I contemplated picking up the phone and returning the call. But if I did that, there'd be a chance I'd throw caution to the wind and not care about his separation. But I guess there'd always be that chance. This man's presence was indeed one of my weaknesses. But how could that be? We've only really been around each other a few times. Ok, that settled it, I was not going to call him back, it was too risky and I needed time to recover from my relationship with Jake. I couldn't afford to be risky right now. So, I opted not to call. Again.

Straight No Chaser: The Beginning

Another late day at the office meant another late run. Before it got completely dark I got in a few miles around the neighborhood. By the time I had gotten back home a car, other than mine, was sitting in my driveway. It was Jake. I rolled my eyes because he showed up unannounced. That's my biggest peeve and he knew it. I ran into the drive way, out of breath, and stopped at his car. After realizing I was at his window, he put his phone down and got out of the car.

Needless to say I was bothered by his lack of calling before showing up at my house. And he knew it.

"How long have you been sitting out here?" I asked, out of breath.

"Fifteen minutes maybe. I know you don't like unannounced visits," he said.

So, he did remember that.

I cut him off mid-sentence, "So, why'd you show up without a phone call first then?"

"But I wanted to see you and you hadn't really been taking my calls," Jake said.

"Ok, still no reason to just show," I said. "So, what's up?"

"Truth. I miss you, Zen. I've been thinking. I want us to try again."

I was stretching and trying to cool down from my run. Working on that project at work really had me stressed and his showing up didn't help.

I saw his lips moving but surely he didn't say what I think he said.

"Excuse me?" I asked with a confused look on my face.

"Zen, let's…try again," he repeated.

"Yeah, that's not going to happen."

"Why not, Zen? We're perfect for each other."

"Perfect. You obviously didn't think that when you were cheating on me. Clearly…" I said.

"Zen, I've apologized for that over and over again. I shouldn't have cheated. I'm sorry, but I know you're who I want to be with," he pleaded.

"Really? Interesting." I said walking towards my front door.

Jake was following me like I was going to let him come inside. I turned around abruptly and glared at Jake.

"Ummm, and you're going where?" I asked.

"I thought you were going to invite me inside so we could finish our conversation," he said.

"The conversation is finished," I told him. "You had your chance and, yeah, you messed it up. I may have forgiven you for cheating, but that does not mean I've forgotten or that I would be crazy enough to trust you again. Now, if you'll excuse me."

I shut the door. With my back against the door, I didn't move until I heard his car start. I looked through the peephole to be sure he was gone. I walked into the kitchen to check on any missed calls and for a bottle of water.

No missed calls.

As I was warming my dinner, I couldn't believe Jake just showed up. He knows it's a peeve of mine to show without calling first, but then to show up and try to talk to me about foolishness?

I deserved better than someone who thought it was okay to cheat and lie to me. I had been working on forgiving him so I could move forward with my life. I hadn't let everything go yet; that situation showed me I needed to work harder. I finished my dinner, showered and started working on my project.

This was going to be a long night.

Chapter 15

After putting in what seemed like a thousand hours the previous week, I thought I was about to see the light at the end of the tunnel. The legal team was going to steer the project from here on out and all I needed to do was oversee things from this point.

I was actually excited going into work today. I could finally take my foot off the peddle a little.

On the way to work I called my mom since I hadn't spoken to her in a while.

"Hey, Ma, how are you?" I asked.

"Hey, stranger, I'm good," she responded.

"How's Dad doing?" I asked.

"Oh, he's good. He just left for work," she responded. We missed you at church," she added.

"Yes, ma'am, I've been working long hours on an acquisition I'm leading and I hadn't made time to breathe," I told her.

"Okay, I figured as much. How's your health?" she asked.

"My health is good, still running, of course, and trying to watch what I eat," I responded.

"Good, good…keep it up," she said.

I snickered a little.

Straight No Chaser: The Beginning

"Well, maybe you'll make it to church this Sunday and we'll get lunch afterwards," she said.

My mom was funny, that was not her asking and her tone was one where she dared you to say no.

"Yes ma'am." I responded.

"Speaking of church, I hadn't seen that handsome young man I saw you talking to the other week," she said.

"Ma, why are looking for him again, did I miss something?" I asked.

"Girl, hush I'm trying to get you married," she said.

Little did she know I was trying to avoid him because he was already married.

"Okay, mom, but I'm not trying to rush marriage. Isn't that what you're always telling me?" I asked.

"Yes, chile, but it's good to have some coals in the fire getting ready," she said.

I laughed and said, "Okay, Ma, I hear you. I'm pulling into work. I'll call you guys later."

"Okay, baby, have a good day," she said as we disconnected.

I was gathering my things and my phone rang. I thought it was my mom again having forgotten to tell me something. I glanced at my phone before answering and saw it was Mr. Handsome. Really? Oh my God, this guy was not letting up. I sent him to voice mail this time and rushed into the building to get ready for my meeting with the legal team.

"Good morning Sarah," I said as I rushed by her desk into my office.

I looked up and saw she brought in a cup of coffee from Black Bean.

"Oh, my God! Thank you! You are a God-send!" I said.

"No problem. Okay, your meeting is at 10 AM and Isaiah called you a few minutes ago," she said.

I looked at her and simply said, "Okay. No disturbances. Due to this big meeting with our legal team, I'll need your hands helping me with copying this report. Just in case, make ten copies for me and place it in a report binder for me with the clear cover."

"Okay, anything else?" she asked.

"No, that's it. I have to double-check one page and I'll get this to you in a bit," I said.

I got right to work, so I'd have everything ready by 9:30 AM. As I was looking over my last report, my cell phone started to vibrate. I looked over at it and saw it was Isaiah.

"Isaiah, I definitely cannot talk to you right now," I said out loud.

I sent the report to Sarah so she could work her magic. This gave me a chance to relax a little before the meeting started. I sat on the couch and leaned back and whispered a prayer.

As I finished my prayer Sarah came in with ten perfect copies ready for the legal team. I was nervous and excited. Excited to get this over with and nervous due to this being my first project and I wanted to make a good impression. Sarah sat the reports on the table in front of me.

"Sarah, sit with me. I'm a nervous wreck," I admitted. We don't have to talk, just sit with me for a few minutes." I said.

"Hmmm ok." she said looking at me strangely.

I'm sure I was freaking her out right now, but I wanted to be calm before going into this meeting. So, I sat there with my eyes closed. Sarah interrupted the quietness of the room.

"Xenia, it's time for you make your way to the conference room," she said at a whisper. And don't worry, you got this," she assured me.

"You're right, I worked my butt off. I got this," I said pumping myself up.

I grabbed my things and headed to the conference room walking confidently. When I got there, I saw I was first to arrive. I scattered my positive vibes into the atmosphere.

While looking out over the city, I heard the door open and a male voice said, "There she is, the woman of the hour."

Straight No Chaser: The Beginning

As I turned around to greet the team, I had to quickly gain my composure. I knew I'd be working with lawyers from this point forward, but what I wasn't expecting was for Isaiah to be one of those lawyers.

I smiled as I was being introduced.

"Xenia, this Isaiah. He'll be heading the legal side of things. You two will be working closely together going forward," my boss said.

"Nice to meet you, Xenia," Isaiah said as he shook my hand.

This man was too fine!

"Likewise," I said as I grabbed my seat.

I passed out the reports and noticed it would only be three of us working on the project. Thank God because working one-on-one wasn't going to fly.

I breezed through my presentation with no problems; everyone seemed pleased, especially with the numbers.

"Are there any questions?" I asked the group.

I looked around the room with a smile on my face, waiting for any questions they may have had. Surprisingly, no one had questions.

"Great!" I exclaimed.

Isaiah looked across the table at me with his beautiful smile.

Straight No Chaser: The Beginning

"Well, Xenia, I look forward to working with you."

I nodded in agreement.

"I understand the goal is to have this acquisition completed in the next few weeks?" Isaiah's associate asked the team.

We all said in unison, "Yes!"

"Okay, well, it looks as though we have our work cut out for us. I propose we get started working right away," his associate said.

I glanced over at Isaiah and said, "I have no objections to that. Feel free to stop by my office before leaving, so we can sync calendars with tentative dates to meet."

I was trying my hardest not to let on that Isaiah and I knew each other already. I started to feel sweat on my upper lip. This was just awesome; beads of sweat on my lip. I already knew underneath my suit jacket the sweat was showing through my shirt. Yuck!

We were in the conference room making sure all goals were communicated for this acquisition. After the meeting was over I invited Isaiah and his associate to my office to look over our calendars. When we reached Sarah's desk, I introduced everyone.

When I said Isaiah's name, Sarah quickly glanced at me. When she caught my eye I immediately shook my head and smiled.

"Sarah, hold my calls for about 15 minutes," I told her while walking into my office.

Straight No Chaser: The Beginning

I sat at my desk to looked at my calendar.

"Would either of you like a bottle of water?" I asked.

They both declined. We began to compare calendars.

"I think we should meet more on the front end, then as we near our deadline, we can possibly taper off," I said.

Isaiah's associate excused himself from the room to take a call. I started sweating again.

"Okay, so, what does your next week look like?" I asked Isaiah.

"You look so beautiful today," he said.

"I don't think that's a day on the calendar. Come on Isaiah. Please let's be professional here. What does your next week look like? This way it'll give you time to look over the report again and you can begin drafting this week," I said.

"It pays to answer my calls. When I heard I would be working with your firm, I called to let you know, to no avail," he said.

"So, you couldn't leave that on voicemail?" I asked.

"I wanted to personally deliver the news," he said smiling.

"Well, I apologize. Now you see why I didn't answer. I've been working my butt off for weeks on this," I said.

"And it shows—you gave an awesome presentation back there."

Straight No Chaser: The Beginning

"Thanks, Isaiah," I said relaxing a bit.

"We don't have to wait for Glen. I'll give him the dates so he can adjust," Isaiah said.

"Ok, great!" I replied.

We agreed on tentative dates for the next few weeks. By the time we were finished Glen came back in the office with a huge grin on his face.

Isaiah and I both looked at each other, then back at Glen.

"Okay, did someone you know win the lottery? You look beyond excited," I said.

"Oh God! Yes, my girlfriend's contractions are getting closer!" he exclaimed.

When he said that I zoned out and thought to myself...Great, I'm going to have to work with Isaiah alone after all.

"That's wonderful." trying to sound excited. Go, be with her!" I told him.

"I hate to do this on such a big project," Glen said.

"Glen, we understand. Family first. Now, get your things and go be with your woman. Congrats man," Isaiah said.

Glen gathered his things and quickly walked out of the office.

Isaiah turned and looked at me.

"Okay, we have our dates penciled in, so I guess we're done here for the day?" he asked.

"Yes, I'll have Sarah to email both you and Glen calendar invites later today," I told him.

"I knew I'd get you to myself sooner or later," he said.

"Isaiah…" I said.

He interrupted me, "It doesn't matter if this is business or not. I told you I wanted to get to know you better, Xenia."

I looked up and saw Sarah at the door.

"Thank you, Isaiah, we shall see each other next week," I said as I extended my hand for him to shake.

He grabbed my hand and kissed it lightly. I wanted to melt.

"Until we meet again…" he said. He walked out of my office, passing by Sarah. "Sarah, it was nice to have met you. We'll be seeing a lot of each other over the next few weeks."

"Nice to have met you as well," Sarah said, shaking his hand.

When he disappeared behind the door I collapsed in my seat. Sarah walked over to my desk and sat down and stared at me. I knew what she was dying to say.

"Go ahead…" I said.

"You wouldn't take HIS phone calls!? OH EM GEE!!!! I mean this with all due respect. Are you crazy!?" she asked.

All I could do was shake my head.

"I mean, Xenia, he's beyond handsome. That smile melted my heart. He has the prettiest teeth!" she said.

"Yes, Sarah, I know."

"Wait, did you know he was going to be working with you?" she asked.

"Yep, found out at 10 AM this morning. Totally caught me off guard," I said.

Okay, now, we must get back to work."

This conversation needed to end. NOW!

"Here are the dates for our meetings. Make sure you send meeting invites to both Isaiah and Glen and copy the Management Team as well," I told her.

"Okay, will do. But, Xenia, we're not done," she said pointing at me.

"Oh…but we are," I said laughing.

"Xenia, you're no fun," Sarah said.

"Awe, I know," I said playfully.

Chapter 16

Our first meeting came quickly and I was so nervous, I couldn't sleep the night before. This meeting was a working lunch, so, I ordered Thai for us and had it delivered to the office.

I asked Sarah to sit in with us in case Isaiah decided he wanted to try something. I didn't know if Glen was going to be at the meeting or not due to the baby.

"Sarah, if Glen is here, you won't need to sit in on the meeting," I told her.

"You just don't want to be with him alone. You're not fooling me," she said smiling. "It's okay, I probably wouldn't trust myself around him either."

"Hush!" I said laughing. "I just need to be sure everything is on the up and up during our meetings, that's all. We, well...*he*, needs to stay focused."

"Okay. All jokes aside, I do understand," she said.

She went back out to her desk and reappeared twenty minutes later with Isaiah and Glen. I looked up from my work and smiled.

"Good afternoon, gentlemen," I said. We all shook hands. "Glen, it's nice to see you, I didn't know if I were going to see you today or not. How's the baby?"

"Beautiful baby boy..." he said gushing. "Head full of hair."

Straight No Chaser: The Beginning

"He got the hair from mom, I assume?" I asked jokingly.

Everyone laughed.

"Yeah, I am lacking in the hair department," he said.

Sarah came back into the office with lunch and she set it up on the table in front of the couch for us.

"Sarah, don't forget to fix yourself a plate as well before you go," I said.

"Xenia, you are in a wonderful mood, I see" Isaiah said.

He hadn't called me since last week.

"Yes, today's a good day," I said. Well, let's dig in. I don't know about you, but I'm starving."

We decided to eat first then got to work. I realized this was going to be a long afternoon.

After going over legal briefs all afternoon my brain was fried…literally. By this time, it was 4 PM and we had gone way over our 2 hour meeting block. But that only meant we were ahead of schedule and would require less at our next meeting. Hopefully.

"Okay, guys, we've been working nonstop this afternoon, how about we call it a day and come back together at our next scheduled time?" Glen said.

I was relieved when he spoke up. Glen read my facial expression on how happy I was about him speaking up.

"Oh my God, Glen, thank you!" I said laughing. I'm hungry again and my brain is toast. I think I'm an intelligent human being but these legal briefs, my goodness." They both laughed at me.

"I'm serious, guys. Legal-eeze, I definitely do not speak," I said.

Isaiah spoke in agreeance, "Okay, we'll organize what was done today and come back together next week."

"Sounds good to me," I said while I was cleaning up from lunch.

"Xenia, let me help you with that," Isaiah said.

"Oh, I got it and what I don't get, I'm sure Sarah can get it," I said.

"Okay, Ms. Xenia," Isaiah said.

We were staring at each other for a moment until Glen broke the silence by clearing his throat.

"Alright, well, if we're done here I'm going to head out and start on revisions tonight," Glen said.

"Glen, kiss the baby for me," I said.

I didn't know what else to say since he obviously caught Isaiah and I staring each other down.

"Yeah, I can't wait to get home and play with him. Although he's still keeping us up at night, he's just so adorable. I can't wait until he gets bigger," he said gushing.

Straight No Chaser: The Beginning

"Awe, yeah, they say enjoy this stage," I said.

"Okay, you guys have a good night," Glen said disappearing behind the door.

What I didn't want to happen happened. Myself and Isaiah in the same room alone and he didn't look as if he was in a hurry to leave. I saw he sat back down on the couch looking over some notes.

"You can stop pretending now," I said.

"Pretending? What are you talking about?" Isaiah said.

I gave him a quick side eye.

"You can stop pretending to read over your notes," I said still cleaning my office.

He laughed, "Okay, you got me."

"Why don't you want to be alone with me, Xenia?" he asked.

"And what makes you think I don't want to be?" I asked.

"Your body language. It changed as soon as Glen left. Look, I'm not going to bite you. Xenia, I like your company and all I want to do is get to know you better."

I've heard that line plenty of times before and even fell for it a few times. I kept cleaning and I heard him get up from the couch. I turned around. By this time we were standing face to face. I took a step back.

"Isaiah, please, this is my place of work," I said.

I turned to clean up the last of the plates and food. My heart was racing and I could feel my upper lip moist from sweat. I hate he made me feel like this.

"You're right," he said. "I apologize, but there's something about you I just can't get enough of. I know whatever this is between us, you feel it too."

He was right, I did feel it, but I was not going to let him know. At least not right now. And if I did let him know, this was not the time. And it was time for him to leave my office.

"Isaiah, I'm flattered, I really am, but this will not happen. It's unprofessional," I said. "I don't appreciate being put in this position."

Isaiah stood there, staring at me. He didn't say a word. I walked to my desk so there would be a barrier between us.

He walked over and stood opposite of me. He looked me in my eyes and smiled and said, "You win…today."

Inside I breathed a sigh of relief. I looked away from him quickly tidying up my office.

I was saved when Sarah walked back into the office.

"You two okay in here?" she inquired smiling.

"Yes, Sarah, I'm actually getting ready to head out so I can go over what all was done here today," Isaiah replied.

"Oh, leaving so soon?" I asked sarcastically.

Straight No Chaser: The Beginning

I was hoping not to let on to Sarah any of our mini-confrontation before she stepped into the office.

Isaiah shook his head at me and smiled, "Yes ma'am, there's no need for me to stick around. I actually have a long night ahead of me."

"Okay, sounds good to me. I'll walk you out," I said.

I waited for Isaiah to gather the last of his things and we began to walk towards the door.

"It was a pleasure, Xenia," Isaiah smirked.

"Likewise."

That's actually all I could muster up to say at the moment. I cleared my throat as I gazed at him deeply, like I was in a trance or something. My trance was then broken by Sarah clearing her throat.

"Okay, well, you have a good evening and have fun going over what was done today," I said sarcastically.

"Yes ma'am, I sure will. You guys have a wonderful evening," he said.

I quickly walked back into my office and closed the door. I sat at my desk and swiveled around in my chair facing the view of the city.

As I sat there, I thought this was way too much pressure for one person to handle. Yes, the man was attractive. But, could I really go there with him while we're working on this project together? I thought I was playing it cool, but now he knew for sure I was feeling him and wanted him as bad as he wanted me.

"DANG IT," I said out loud.

Sarah came back in the office.

"Zen, you okay?" she asked.

"What, yeah. Yeah, I'm fine Sarah. Why do you ask?" I inquired.

She looked at me like I had three heads.

"Because you said 'dang it' really loud! I thought you hurt yourself or something," she said.

"Oh, yeah, I'm fine girl."

I laughed, trying to play it off.

She looked at me strangely, nodded her head, pursed her lips and walked back to her desk closing the door behind her.

I must have been really loud, especially if she jumped up and came to see about me.

"Okay, Zen, get it together, girl," I thought to myself. I stood up from the chair and scanned my office to see what I needed to take home with me to work on for the night.

I packed my bag with my laptop and the notes from our meeting and turned the lights off in my office.

Straight No Chaser: The Beginning

As I opened the door to my reception area, Sarah swiveled around in her chair and just looked at me with a smile on her face.

I looked up from my phone and saw Sarah's expression.

"Umm, what's wrong with you?" I asked slowly.

"Oh, nothing…nothing at all," she said with a smirk on her face.

"Yeah, right. Spill it, what's up?" I asked.

She adjusted herself in her chair and asked, "You like him don't you?"

I felt myself becoming uncomfortable. I didn't know what to say, so I said the first dumb thing that came to mind.

"What? Who are you talking about?" I asked.

Sarah gave me that 'you know who the heck I'm talking about look.'

I looked at her and smacked my lips and said "Uh, no, I do not." At this point, I was trying my best to get out of the office as fast as I could.

"Uh-huh," she said, shaking her head. Zen, it's okay, he's a handsome guy and he seems to be one of the good ones."

"Why is that Sarah, because he's a lawyer or have you been talking to him behind my back?" I asked.

"No, not talking to him, but I pick up on body language and his body language says a lot when he's around you," Sarah said.

I didn't let her know this, but I picked up on his body language as well and read the same.

"Okay, Sarah…not your business. I'll see *you* in the morning!" I said walking away.

Sarah laughed and said, "You only say that when I'm right, you know that right?"

"Good night, lady!" I said getting on the elevator.

As the elevator door closed I fell against the back wall and let out a deep sigh. I was so glad this day was over and done with.

As I was walking to my car, my phone began to ring. I looked down and saw it was Jake.

"Oh my god, Jake, I can't deal with you right now!" I said out loud. I let his call go to voicemail. I got in the car and sat there for a few moments reflecting over the last thirty minutes of my work day.

I realized that if I continued to allow what went on today, especially for as long as it did, I'd be in a heap of trouble— sooner rather than later. All I could do was shake my head at myself. I was in control of this situation, no one else. Me.

At that moment, I knew a gym date was in my future. I badly needed to sort through this mess!

Chapter 17

The acquisition was almost complete and I could not be any happier about it. This meant, no more late nights or early mornings. No more being the last one out of my department most evenings. No more overtime. I'd have my not-so-social life back!

But, at the same time I couldn't help but to think that I wouldn't see Isaiah on a regular basis any more. Well, technically, I could. BUT. Yeah, no. I had to keep reminding myself he was still married and I didn't need that type of drama or any drama for that matter in my life.

Today, we were meeting for the last time before meeting with the company and the rest of the managers. It was crunch time. Everything looked good and we thought everyone involved would approve.

"Sarah, could you come in here please!" I yelled from inside my office.

"Yes ma'am, what can I do you for?" she asked.

I was still looking down at the spreadsheets when she came in. I said not skipping a beat, "Don't forget to have pastries and coffee in the conference room tomorrow for the meeting."

"Yes ma'am, I placed the order this morning and I'll pick it up on the way to work in the morning," she said.

"Awesome!" I said still looking at the spreadsheets.

"Zeeeeennnn," Sarah said singing my name.

She broke my concentration and I looked up at her.

"Hey, girl, you alright?" Sarah asked.

"I'm sorry," I said. "This acquisition has been all over the place. I apologize. After tomorrow, the old me will be back."

Sarah smiled and said, "Yeah...okay!" She laughed as she walked out of my office.

I sat on the couch in my office and took in a deep breath to try and calm my nerves. When that didn't work, I got up and walked over to the window and just gazed outside looking over the city's skyline.

I don't know why I was stressing out the way I was; I had gone over the spreadsheets more than enough times to know that everything was going to be fine and everyone involved would be happy.

I don't know why, but I decided to call Isaiah. Maybe he could calm my nerves. I picked up my office phone and sat at my desk looking at the dial pad...still contemplating dialing his number. I had the receiver up to my ear so long until the phone started to make that annoying buzzing sound. I hung up the phone. I sat there again shaking my head at myself while, at the same time, laughing at myself.

I don't know what it was about this man, but as of recently, I couldn't keep him off my mind. No matter what I did—going for runs, going to the gym, he was even showing up in my dreams now! The more I tried to put him out of my head, the more he showed up. UNINVITED!

Sarah buzzed my office phone.

"Yes ma'am," I said.

"Xenia, Isaiah is on the line for you," she replied.

Are you kidding me? See what I mean? I think of him and somehow he shows up. This was beginning to freak me out even more.

"Thanks, Sarah, send him through," I told her. Well, hello there, Sir. Let me tell you something funny." I didn't even give him the opportunity to say hello.

"I was just about to call you," I said.

"Beat ya to it!" he responded laughing.

"Yes, you did," I said. So, what do you have for me? Please do not tell me there is some problem that has popped up at the last minute," I said.

"No problem at all. I was actually just calling to check on you. I know this is your first big project in your new role and I wanted to see how your nerves were holding up," he said.

"Truth moment—I am freaked out of my mind! That's actually why I was going to call you. In hopes that you could calm my nerves. I've looked over those spreadsheets one hundred times this morning," I said laughing.

"Oh, really now? YOU were calling ME to calm you down? I am shocked and surprised," he said.

"Yeah, yeah, yeah. I surprise people sometimes, Isaiah. I'm not as bad as you think," I said.

"Nope, I don't think you're bad at all. I do think you're way too guarded," he said.

The phone went silent. It seemed like forever. He was right. I was guarded. But who could blame me after how my relationship with Jake ended. Granted all men aren't like that, but come on, give me some slack.

"Hello?" Isaiah said.

"I'm here. Maybe I am too guarded. But, you know sometimes a girl has to be, Isaiah."

"I understand. I have to be honest, since I've been separated, I'm a little guarded. But, I don't let it consume my life and keep me from getting to know people," he said.

He had a point.

"Well, it takes me a while to allow people into my space. I take that very serious, so if I allow it, I hate when people don't treat it as a gift," I told him.

"I totally get that. I'm the same way. Contrary to what you may want to think of me, I don't have a huge circle of friends I interact with. Especially since I moved here; but back at home, I didn't have a lot of friends either," he said.

Man, I felt comfortable talking to him. My nerves had actually calmed down considerably and I was uber-glad about that.

"Xenia, I hate to do this, but let's talk business for a few moments. Did you have any questions about the contracts that were sent over by the messenger?" Isaiah asked.

"Uh, no. No, everything looked good. I even understood what I was reading this time," I said as we both laughed.

"Good! We made a lot of progress over the past few weeks I see," he said.

"Sure did." I said. "I'm actually excited about being able to understand these contracts now," I said.

"I see you are. You caught on pretty quickly," he said.

Sarah peaked her head into the office and I motioned for her to come in.

"Isaiah, can you hold on for a second please?" I asked him.

"Sure thing…" he replied.

"Zen, I hate to interrupt your phone call, but I need your signature for this package that's going out today," Sarah said.

"Oh sure, hold a second," I told her.

I took Isaiah off hold, "Hey Isaiah, I have to go. Do you mind if I call you back later?" I asked.

"Not at all, Xenia. But before you go, how about we meet for lunch today?" he asked.

I froze. I couldn't say anything. I must have had a panicked look on my face because Sarah's facial expression changed as if she were asking if I were okay, without saying a word.

"Ummm, let me get back with you on that," I said. I hurried and hung up the phone without saying goodbye.

I couldn't believe I hung up on him like that! I know he must've thought I was some kind of crazy woman. Heck, I thought I was a crazy woman!

"You know you didn't have to get off the phone with him, right? All I needed was your signature right there," she said as she pointed to the one line.

I shook my head and said, "Yeah, it's okay. I needed to get off the phone anyway."

"Okay, Xenia…" she said shaking her head at me.

"What? What is it now?" I asked.

She took a deep breath, like she was carefully choosing her words.

"You know you want to go out with that man. I don't know why you keep playing around. He keeps asking you out and you keep dodging him. One day he's not going to ask anymore," she said.

I didn't like anything she said, but she had a point.

"Sarah…" I said.

She stood there looking for me to say something smart. I didn't. She walked out.

This can't be my life right now. It felt like I was stuck between a rock and hard place concerning Isaiah. I didn't know what to do! If I go out with him, I could possibly fall for him; which is not ideal due to him still being married. If I don't go out with him, I could potentially miss out on getting to know someone that could be a pretty good friend. But now the question is can men and women really be friends and nothing more?

This was too much for me to handle. I wasn't thinking clearly at all.

I picked up my cell phone to call Amy.

While I was dialing her number a text from Amy came through.

"Girl, call me!!!!!!!! ☺"

"GIRL!!!!!!!!!!!!!!!!!!!!!!! Guess what? No, you'll never guess! He asked me to go to Jamaica!" she exclaimed.

A smile came across my face instantly.

"What!? Your first trip together? Or am I so out of the loop, that I've missed your first trip?" I asked.

"No, this is our first trip. He's asked before, but I was a little uncomfortable going since we didn't know each other that well," Amy said.

"You told him yes, right?" I asked.

"But of course! I need to go swimsuit shopping like yesterday…" she said. "You down this weekend?"

"But of course sistah! I wouldn't miss a shopping trip like this for anything in the world," I assured her.

By this time I almost forgot I was calling her for advice. But I didn't want to bring her down with my crazy story.

As Amy was telling me about her trip, I zoned out for a bit thinking about Isaiah. What if I were making a mistake not getting to know him? What if I needed him in my life? I know he's separated, but what if he's the man of my dreams? I did tell myself I would do things differently when I decided to date again.

"Zen. Zen! You still there?" Amy asked.

"Girl, yeah, I'm here. I'm sorry," I said. I zoned out for a minute. You have my undivided attention. When are you guys leaving again?"

There was a brief second of dead air.

"Zen baby, talk to me. What's going on?" Amy asked.

I knew it. I was about to bring this positive vibe down with my crazy.

"Amy, I don't want to talk about it right now," I said.

"Yeah, well…whatever. Talk," she demanded.

I let out a deep sigh and rattled off my situation with Isaiah. After bringing her up to speed on everything, I braced myself for her response. Some days she was straight, no chaser, and other days I couldn't call it.

"Zen, you're like a sister to me. So, girl, don't mess with this man. Yes, he's separated, but, he's still married…" she said. I don't care how much he wants to tell you his sob story about how things are going bad with his marriage, don't fall for it!" Amy begged.

I know everything she was saying was true, but part of me honestly didn't care. Part of me now wanted to get to know him. I don't know why, but I just did.

"Okay, that's all I needed to hear," I said.

I could feel Amy's side eye through the phone.

"Zen..." Amy said sternly.

"Amy, don't worry. I'm good," I assured her.

"Okay…" she said slowly.

"Alright, girl, I'm serious don't worry. I'll see you this weekend. Now I have to go and finish preparing for this meeting," I told her.

We disconnected the phone and I sat in my office in silence, replaying what Amy said. Nothing good would come of me and Isaiah. Nothing at all.

I picked up the spreadsheets once more and began to scrutinize them..

I never called Isaiah.

Chapter 18

The day finally arrived. I was nervous, exhausted and felt nauseous. I didn't sleep the night before. I think I may have gotten two hours the entire night.

I pulled myself out of bed to get ready for work. I'm glad the meeting wasn't until mid-morning. This would give me enough time to gather my thoughts after getting to the office. That also meant I didn't have to rush to the office. Sarah was taking care of the pastries and coffee. I just needed to calm my nerves.

I walked into the kitchen half asleep to start my coffee pot. I walked back into my room to pick out an outfit. I had to look professional but chic at the same time. I decided to go with my black and white suit and for the added touch, I chose my new purple pumps.

I walked back into the kitchen to fix my first cup of coffee. I knew this was going to be the first of many today. While I was in the kitchen I turned on the radio to really get myself moving. I turned it to my favorite morning show, and they were talking about love and relationships.

I walked back into my room to hop in the shower. When I walked back into my room I decided to check my phone to see if any work emails had come through.

My message indicator light was blinking and I saw that I missed a text from Isaiah.

Straight No Chaser: The Beginning

Hey Zen. Just wanted to send you good vibes for today's meeting. See ya soon.

I smiled at the text and decided to respond later because it was getting late and jumped in the shower.

After rushing to get out of the house on time, I sat in the car for a few minutes to catch my breath. I was starting to sweat a little and I needed to cool off. My phone went off again and I grabbed it to see who was texting me.

Jake.

Hey Zen. We haven't spoken in a while ☹ I wanted to check to see how you were doing. Hit me back when you have the chance.

Okay, Jake, I definitely don't have the time for you right now. I put the phone down and started the car. Then I realized I hadn't responded to Isaiah's text. I picked the phone up again and responded to him. It was short and to the point. We'd see each other later this morning.

When I finally got in to work, I had another coffee in hand from Black Bean. I was surprisingly not rushing into my office. I think I had finally calmed down or my coffee had finally kicked in.

I normally zoom past Amy's desk and into my office but today I stopped to say good morning. Even she was surprised.

I placed my things down on my desk and took a deep breath and let the last of my nerves go.

There was a knock on my office door and when I looked up, I saw it was Isaiah and Glen. They were early!

I smiled at them both and said, "Gentlemen, please come in!"

They proceeded to come in and sat down on the couch.

"Are you ready, Xenia?" Glen asked.

"You know, yes, I am. I couldn't sleep last night, but my coffee has finally kicked in and I am ready to knock this out of the park! Then, I will celebrate tonight by relaxing," I said.

"Relaxing sounds good," Isaiah said. Then drinks it is after work. We can all meet at the bar down the street from here."

"Sounds good to me," I said. Lord knows I needed a stiff drink to take the edge off.

"I'll have to pass on this one," Glen said. I have to pick up the little guy tonight."

Great! Glen let me down. I was going to use him as a buffer. Now, it was only going to be myself and Isaiah. Nice. I think this was a set up.

"Awe," I said disappointingly. Well, we will certainly toast to you. How is the little guy, anyway?"

"He is awesome. Other than us losing sleep, he is doing very well," Glen said smiling from ear to ear.

Straight No Chaser: The Beginning

"That's great to hear." I tried not to sound too disappointed that he was leaving us high and dry later. I just needed to stay on my *pee's and que's*. I'm sure Isaiah was happy that it would just be me and him for happy hour. Maybe I would invite Sarah. I'll figure that out later.

"Alright, guys, the day is here, so let's get down to business," I said excitedly.

I glanced over at Isaiah and he looked a little perplexed. I ignored it for the moment, but if he continued to look like that, I would need to make sure he was okay before our meeting.

We looked over everything and organized the flow of the presentation. We were set and we had an hour before the meeting began.

I excused myself from the office to be sure the conference room was set up to my liking. I knew I didn't have to check behind Amy, she had been working with me long enough to know how I liked things.

When I came back into the office, I saw Sarah had made copies of the materials needed for the meeting. I glanced over them once more and had her place them in the conference room on the table.

"It looks like everything is going smoothly so far. All we have to do is answer all of the hard questions and we'll be in the clear," I exclaimed.

After sitting and shooting the breeze for a few minutes to take our minds off the meeting, we walked towards the conference room where everyone was already in place. My nerves started up again.

Somehow I think Isaiah could tell.

He whispered in my ear, "It's okay, I got you."

He didn't know what that did to me. A nice looking man whispering anything in my ear…yeah, not good!

I looked back at him and smiled and walked into the conference room. I introduced Glen and Isaiah to everyone in the room. The presentation was a blur! I don't remember one word I said during that hour. I don't remember one word Isaiah said during that hour. All I know is, the acquisition was approved and I got praises from the Management team.

Thank you Jesus!!

After shaking hands with my bosses, we all agreed on going out to lunch to celebrate that afternoon. Isaiah and Glen had to pass on lunch, as they were working on another project for their firm.

"So, Xenia, I will see you later," Isaiah asked as we walked back to my office.

I turned my head slightly towards him and said, "Yes, you shall. Maybe I should invite Sarah, since she helped out a little."

I looked at him to see if I could read the facial expression on his face. He looked a little disappointed.

"Sarah, would you like to meet for drinks after work with Isaiah and myself?" I asked.

Sarah glanced at Isaiah as I was eyeing her.

"You know what, I can't. I have a date tonight," she said.

Thanks a lot, Sarah!

"Oh, okay, well, have a good time on your date!" I said. We'll talk about that later."

She gave me a bashful look and started working again.

I glanced at Isaiah who now had a smirk on his face. This felt like another set up! How did I keep falling for these today?

"Sarah, I'm going to lunch with the Management Team and I will be back afterwards. I will walk these two down." I told her.

"Gotcha," she said.

"You actually can take off an hour early today for helping us out," I told her.

I knew she'd be happy, especially since she had a "date" later. I bet anything she didn't have a date.

"Really!? Awesome!" she said.

"After you," Isaiah said, pointing to the elevator.

"Thank you," I said.

After walking them both to the lobby, I was eager to get to my car, because I was famished and I was ready for lunch with my team!

Glen parted ways first and that left me and Isaiah in the parking lot…alone. What is it with everyone today not being on my side? I'm trying to be strong and not give in to this man, but everyone is getting out of my way to do just that! UGH!!!

I looked at Isaiah and smiled.

"Well, I better get going so I can meet my team for lunch, I'm starving," I said. I guess we'll see each other for Happy Hour right?"

Isaiah looked at me and smiled.

"What is it?" I asked.

"Oh, nothing, Xenia. I'm just taking you all in," he said.

"Taking me all in?" I asked.

"Yep, don't act coy with me. I'm just feeling you out that's all," he said. And, yes, Happy Hour, I will definitely see you then."

He walked away and got into his car. I stood there watching him drive him away. Don't ask me why. I know he was watching me, watch him! UGH!!!!

I walked over to my car and got in. While I was opening the door, my phone rang. I looked down and it was Mama.

I hadn't spoken with her in forever because of this project, so I picked up the phone.

"Hey, Mama!" I said excited to hear from her.

"Hey, Zen, girl!! I know today was supposed to be the end of your project and I was just calling to see how it went. But I'm sure it went well with you working on it," she said.

"Yes ma'am, we presented it today and everyone was pleased. I'm actually on my way to lunch with my Management Team and the Management Team from the company we just helped," I replied.

"Oh, well, look at you!! I'm proud of you, Suga! Keep up the good work. I tried to stay out of your way the past few weeks because I knew you had your plate full and all," she said.

"Awe, thanks, Ma! I appreciate it. Now, I can breathe a little until the next assignment comes up. But, until then, I am going to enjoy my freedom. I'm going shopping with Amy this weekend. I get back on my gym schedule and, more importantly, I can get back to church."

"Yes, chile! We've missed you these past few Sundays. Pastor Anderson asked about you last Sunday. I told him all of what you had going on," she said.

"Okay, well, tell Pastor Anderson 'hello' and I'll see him soon. Okay, Mama, I just pulled up to the restaurant, let me call you back later."

"Okay, baby, bye-bye," she said.

"Bye, Mama."

We disconnected the phone and I realized just how blessed I was. I had a job that was going well, my parents were in good health, my friends were doing well and we were there for each other and I had my health! Life was pretty darn good.

After lunch, I rushed back to the office stuffed! Lunch was amazing and the restaurant we went to, I'd never gone there before, but I will surely be back.

As I was heading into my office, Sarah called my name.

"Xeniaaaaa," she sang my name. "How was lunch? And, more importantly, you are keeping your Happy Hour date, right?"

I looked at her with piercing eyes.

"Yeah, about that," I said. She followed me into my office.

"I know you lied about that date thing tonight," I said. "You are not slick, miss girl."

She laughed.

"It's not funny," I said. "Now I have to be there with him by myself!"

"Zen, it will be okay," Sarah said.

"Yeah, okay. I'm not staying long and I'm only having one drink," I said.

"Zen he's not going to bite," she said.

"Sarah, he's married. Regardless of how he feels, how I feel, nothing changes that fact," I told her.

"Well, okay, you're right," she said.

I knew better, she wasn't going to just give up that easily on this topic.

I finished up my work for the day and as it got closer to the time for me to leave for the day, I felt my stomach turn into knots.

Sarah came to the door smiling.

"Whatever…" I said laughing.

She burst out laughing.

"Hey, I didn't say anything. I just came to let you know I'm heading out since you said I could," she said.

"Have a good date, missy," I said, laughing.

"Oh, I definitely will," she said walking toward the elevator.

I had an hour to get myself together to meet Isaiah for Happy Hour. I was still uneasy and unsure about meeting him. But I guess it was too late. I could come up with an excuse like I always do.

To call or not to call; it's now or never.

Chapter 19

I walked into the bar, nervous, stomach still in knots. I looked around to see if I saw Isaiah sitting at the bar. I saw no signs of him, so I took the first available two seats I saw and waited.

The bartender came over and I ordered a Whiskey Sour, my one drink, while I waited. After twenty minutes, I looked at my phone to see what time it was. This wasn't like him to be late. I sent him a text to make sure everything was okay.

Hey it's Zen, I wanted to be sure we did say celebratory drinks this evening. If so, I'm here....waiting.

I began to grow a little anxious. I never liked the feeling of being stood up, but by someone who has hounded you for a while about going out...

I sat there for fifteen more minutes in hopes I didn't indeed look as if I were being stood up.

That was it. I paid for my drink and left.

I couldn't help but feel a little upset about it. At least when I decided not to go out when he asked, I did call to let him know! But for you to invite me out to celebrate and not show!? Almost unforgivable.

I had to calm myself down; I was jumping to conclusions. Maybe something came up with work. He did say he had to pass on lunch earlier due to having to work on another project. Maybe he was in an accident. Either way, he had some explaining to do. I don't like looking stupid at anyone's expense.

I got in my car and decided to drive home and make dinner, instead of grabbing something on the way. When I pulled into my driveway, my phone rang. I answered without looking to see who it was.

"Hello?" I said.

"Hey, Zen..." the male voice responded.

I paused, and then let out a sigh when I realized who it was.

"Hi Jake. What's up?" I said. Part of me was hoping it were Isaiah with his explanation on standing me up.

"Don't sound so enthused. I was just calling to check up on you," he said.

"I'm sorry. I answered without looking to see who it was," I said. I'm fine, just getting home from work."

"Working late tonight?" he asked.

"Well, not really. I was out celebrating the completion of my project being in my new role," I said.

"Oh. Well, congratulations on that, I know you're excited!" he said.

"Yes, I am actually! I can't wait for more opportunities in the future," I told him. Listen Jake, I'm on my way into the house to fix dinner. Can I call you later?"

"Well, another reason I called was to ask if I could come over? I didn't want to just show up," he said.

"Oh, like you did the last time?" I said, sarcastically.

We both laughed a little.

There was brief silence on the line. What was I going to say?

"Sure," I said.

OH, MY GOSH!!!! What the heck did I just say!? I said it before I even thought about it!

"Wow, really?" he said shockingly.

It was too late to take it back now.

"Yes, you can come over." I said reluctantly. I had to give myself the side eye on this one!

"Ok, well did you need anything?" he asked.

"Now that you ask, you can bring a bottle of wine," I said.

"I know just the bottle." he said and hung up the phone.

Dang it! I wonder why he was asking to come over again and what he felt the need to talk about. I didn't even know what I was going to cook.

I walked into the house and looked around to be sure it was as neat as possible. Regardless of who was coming over, I didn't want them to think I lived in a pigsty.

I walked over to the coffee table and straightened the magazines. I then walked into the kitchen and took out the salmon and asparagus, my favorite.

I had to get out of my work clothes—my feet were killing me from the heels I decided to wear all day and I was more than glad to get out of them.

I changed into some sweat pants and t-shirt. Although I loved the way they fit and looked on me, I rarely wore sweats. But I was home and needed to be comfortable.

I walked back into the kitchen to get started on dinner. I turned on my cooking playlist so I could get in my groove. About twenty minutes into cooking, the doorbell rang. I looked up to see what time it was; he was early.

As I looked through the peephole, I could not believe my eyes. It was Isaiah! What in the world? How did he know where I lived? Do I answer the door? I had my music turned up loud, so he knew for sure I was home.

Here goes nothing! I opened the door with a stern look on my face.

"I'm so sorry about earlier, Zen," he said, apologetically. Something came up that I had to put my focus on and when I got the situation under control, it was way late."

"So, instead of answering my text, you decided to leave me hanging?" I asked.

"Zen, it wasn't like that. Something came up with one of my kids back home that I had to deal with," he said.

I couldn't argue when it came to people's kids. So, I had no choice but to let up a little. Just a little.

"Well, I hope your kid is okay now. But, you still could have responded to the text. It only takes a few seconds," I said.

"I know, I apologize," he said. "Do you mind if I come in so we can finish talking?"

"Actually, I do mind. I have company coming over shortly," I said.

His face changed immediately.

"Besides sir, how did you know where I lived? I don't recall ever telling you," I said.

"Yeah, your mom gave it to me one Sunday after church and told me to stop by to see you. But, I didn't that day because I don't like stopping by people's homes unannounced. But, today I had to see you because of the circumstances," he explained.

Thanks a lot mom! Now, I was going to have to have a conversation with her about giving out my personal information.

"My mom? Nice…" I said.

At this time, Jake was pulling up in the drive way. Isaiah turned around and saw the car pulling in.

"Well, since your company is here, I guess I'll go," he said.

Straight No Chaser: The Beginning

I couldn't believe this guy was trying to sound pitiful. He stood me up! Yes, it was because of the kids, but still; let's be considerate.

"Okay, have a nice night," I said.

Jake made his way to the front door and the look on his face was priceless. He wanted to say something, but yet he looked as though he just wanted to leave the situation alone.

"Hey, Jake, you can come in and put that in the kitchen," I said.

"Okay. Did I interrupt something?" he asked.

"Not really," I replied.

"What's up man, I'm Isaiah," he said. "I was just leaving. Jake, right? We met at the grocery store a few weeks back. Good to see you," he said.

This situation probably should've been awkward for me, but surprisingly it wasn't. I stood there looking at Isaiah, while Jake walked into the house and made himself at home.

"Well, I'll go. Umm, can I give you a call later?" he asked.

"Sure. Talk to you later," I said.

I closed the door and pressed my head against it and closed my eyes. First, how dare he come to my house unannounced? Second, you show up with a sob story. I don't know if the story was true or not, but come on!!

Straight No Chaser: The Beginning

I walked into the kitchen to find my salmon almost done. It smelled great!

"Thanks for the wine," I said.

"You're welcome." Jake said. You sure I didn't interrupt anything a few minutes ago? It kinda looked as if I did."

"Maybe you interrupted *to him*, but it's cool," I said, not missing a beat.

I needed to finish preparing dinner because I was starving at this point.

Jake fixed us both a glass of wine and it was a great pick. I had to give it to him, he picked a great one. This was indeed one of the things I missed about him.

"Well, what's for dinner?" he asked.

"My favorite. Salmon and asparagus!" I said.

"Actually, I've had a taste for salmon for like two weeks now."

"Great. It's a win, then," I said, taking another sip of wine.

Jake sat at the bar looking at me finish dinner. I decided to make dessert as well. Like I needed it, but I made red velvet cupcakes as well.

"You're going all out and making dessert, on a school night?" he said jokingly.

I laughed, "Well, yes. I had a taste for these, too. I'll work it off tomorrow when I go to the gym."

Straight No Chaser: The Beginning

"I can't tell you the last time I went to the gym," he said.

"Really? I'm surprised to hear that, especially when you got me on the routine of going," I said.

"Yeah, well, after we broke up, I stopped doing a lot of things," he said.

Here we go. I knew it. I just wanted to get through this dinner without talking about the break up. I looked up at him and just gave him a blank look. What was I supposed to say after him telling me that?

"Wow." I said as I nodded my head. I turned around to check the salmon. The asparagus was almost done.

"Yep," he said.

There was silence. Nothing but the music playing.

The cupcakes were finally done. I only made a few since it was just the two of us. I sat them on the counter to cool before icing them.

We fixed our plates and finally sat down at the table to eat. Jake did something he never really took charge of before. He blessed our food. After he blessed the food, I gave him this strange look.

"What is it?" he asked.

"You never really took charge of blessing our food. I always had to ask, borderline beg you do it," I said.

"Well, just like I stopped doing some things when we broke up, I started evaluating and doing other things differently," he said.

Who was this man sitting across from me?

"So, are we going to do this? Are we going to take a walk down memory lane tonight? Is this why you wanted to have dinner?" I asked.

"Not really, Zen. I honestly just wanted to see you. And technically, you brought up dinner, not me," he smiled.

"Ha! Yeah, you're right. Okay, I'll give you a pass on that one," I said.

"So, why'd you agree to seeing me tonight after all the other times I asked?" he inquired.

I looked at him after taking a bite of the salmon.

"I don't know to be honest." I looked down at my plate to break our eye contact.

"Well, whatever changed your mind, I'm glad it did."

After we finished eating, I iced the cupcakes and we both ate two each. They were so good!

I had to admit, putting everything to the side with how we ended things, I was actually having a good time. So much so, I didn't look at the time even once.

I lost count of the glasses of wine I had throughout dinner, but I started to really feel tipsy. I knew it was time for him to go home. But, I couldn't just come out and say 'go home'.

I started to clear the table, hoping he'd get the hint. Jake got up as well to help me with the dishes. When we were together he never helped. Maybe he has changed a little.

I walked over to the sink to get the water ready and I felt him close to me. I turned around and he was standing closer than I felt comfortable. But, I couldn't move out of the way.

"Excuse me, Jake."

"Zen…" he said.

"Jake, nope." I said shaking my head. We are not going there tonight."

"Zen, I know you still feel the chemistry between us," he said.

I did. But I think it was the wine.

Then he just went for it. He kissed me. Man, he kissed me. I forgot how it felt to be kissed. I forgot how it felt to be wanted. I forgot. It felt good. After fighting the surprise kiss a few seconds, I gave in.

Chapter 20

I decided on brunch Saturday morning after my workout, so I went to my favorite place to read a book and survey the crowd like I always do.

A few weeks had passed and I hadn't spoken with either Jake or Isaiah. After the kiss with Jake, I had to distance myself from him totally. Although nothing more happened, I couldn't be around him—especially, if there would be alcohol involved.

Isaiah on the other hand, I still couldn't get over the fact he showed up to my house unannounced! The night Jake was over, he called later that night. I didn't answer due to my being in an alcohol-induced slumber.

While I was looking over the menu, I felt someone tap my shoulder. I turned around and...guess who it was?

Isaiah.

I took a deep breath and said, "Well, hello, Isaiah. Wait. Are you stalking me?"

He smiled and said, "I'm fine, Zen. NO! I'm not a stalker."

"That's what all stalkers say," I said. I was hoping he wasn't going to invite himself to sit down.

"You hadn't returned my phone calls over the past few weeks," he said.

"Yes, I know and for good reason," I said.

"Zen, I've apologized for not showing. What else can I do to show you how sorry I am?" he asked.

I looked at him. He looked at me with the saddest eyes. I tilted my head and squinted my eyes at him.

"What? Are you trying to Jedi mind trick me or something?" he asked.

I laughed and said, "Nope. I'm not."

I thought for a second and said, "Have a seat, Isaiah."

I knew I'd regret telling him that.

"I know it seems as though we are always in the same places at the same time, but I assure you, I'm NOT stalking you," he said.

I stared at him and didn't say anything.

"So, you're just going to stare at me and say nothing?" he said.

"Well, I could do that," I said sarcastically.

"Come on, don't be like that. I don't want you upset with me."

"Just FYI, I don't hold grudges," I assured him.

He looked relieved.

"I love this place. This is the only place I actually don't mind sitting outside to eat," I said.

"Why is that?" he asked.

"Honestly, I don't know. I guess it's how they have things set up out here," I said as I glanced at him. "So, I come here when it's nice outside with my book and enjoy the sights."

"That's cool, Zen. So, are we officially having brunch together today since you invited me to have a seat," he asked.

"I guess so," I said with a smirk.

I waved for my waitress to come over to the table.

"Can we have one more menu for this gentleman please?" I asked.

"You're so formal," he said.

I laughed, because it wasn't the first time I'd heard that.

"Yeah. Well, you're in good company. A lot of people think that sometimes. I promise you, I let my hair down at times," I said smiling.

We ordered our food and I was on my second mimosa of the hour and I was feeling pretty good. I had to admit Isaiah was good company. Our conversation was flowing and I almost forgot my reservations for him. Then, his phone rang.

"Excuse me," he said as he answered the phone.

Straight No Chaser: The Beginning

I hate when people answer their phone at the table. It's like what do you do, look the person dead in their face while they're on the phone having a conversation? Do you then take your phone out and begin or pretend to check for imaginary messages?

"Hello? Heeeyy there," he said. Okay. Okay. That sounds good to me. Okay, well, let me call you back, I'm having breakfast with a colleague. Bye"

I couldn't help but smile.

"Colleague huh?" I asked.

"Yes. Aren't we colleagues?" he asked.

"I guess we are," I said.

I had to be honest, I did feel some kind of way being referred to as a colleague. But, that's what we were. That comment also let me know…well… I *assumed* the person on the other end was another woman.

By this time our food had come to our tables. I ordered the Macadamia and Hazel Nut French Toast with scrambled eggs and extra bacon. Isaiah ordered their signature Red Velvet Pancakes.

"I worked out this morning before getting here and I am starving. This is about to be devoured!" I said putting the French Toast in my mouth.

Isaiah laughed and shook his head at me.

"What?" I asked.

"Most women wouldn't tear into their food like that sitting in front of a man," he said.

"Yeah, well, I ain't most women. I love to eat and eat I will," I said laughing and grabbing for my bacon.

"Yeah, I see!" he said laughing.

"Good food, good times." I said. I can't afford to eat like a bird, regardless of who's around me."

"That's good to hear. I hate being around people period who are afraid to be themselves," he said.

"The only time I hold back is if I'm out with my bosses or some sit-down, plated event. Then, my etiquette kicks in." I said.

"Same here," Isaiah said.

I was curious about Isaiah. Since he was sitting across from me unexpectedly, may as well get to know him right?

"So, Isaiah, what's your story?" I asked sipping my drink.

He stopped eating for a second.

"What do you mean, my story? You keep asking me that."

"Like I said, what's your story? Who's the real man behind what I see?" I asked.

"Oh, so, now you want to get to know me?" he said with a smirk.

"Yeah, I guess." I said. Okay, I'm listening."

"Well, you already know why I moved here. You know I'm separated from my wife and hopefully will be filing for divorce soon," he said.

"Have you two tried working it out?" I asked.

"We did, but…" he said.

I cut him off.

"No counseling?" I asked.

"Yeah that was part of trying to work it out, but things still didn't change. Everything was my fault. She didn't want to even look in the mirror at the possibility of anything being her fault," he said.

I almost felt sorry for him.

"That sucks when people refuse to look at the man or woman in the mirror. It's a tough thing to do, but to better oneself daily, I think everyone should do that. Not for others' sake but for your own sake. We can't stay the same forever; I don't think we *should* stay the same forever. Ever changing, ever evolving—isn't that what life is about? Changing? Like, I'm not the same person I was in college, or as I was in high school. If I were, I don't think I'd be as successful as I am today," I said.

"Hey, I totally agree with you. But when you're complacent with where you are in life, what you're doing with your life, you really can't do or say much to change their minds," he said.

Straight No Chaser: The Beginning

I nodded to agree with him and we sat in silence for a minute as we both took bites of our food. I decided to cut myself off from drinking any more mimosas and ordered coffee to sober up before driving home.

"I was wondering when you were going to cut yourself off," Isaiah said with a smile.

"Ha, ha. Very funny. I know when to cut myself off. I can't be in public drunk making a spectacle of myself," I said.

"Yeah, that would be no good. I'd have to disassociate myself with the likes of you," Isaiah said, trying to make me laugh. It worked.

"You're an okay guy, Isaiah."

He looked as much shocked as *I was* saying it.

"I'm sorry, can you say that again?" he smirked.

"Uh, no. I will not." I said laughing. If you didn't hear it the first time, don't count on me repeating myself."

Our waitress came to clear our table and I asked for separate checks.

"No, one check is fine," Isaiah said cutting me off.

"I can't let you do that," I said

"You can and you will," he said.

"Okay, I'll be right back with the check," the waitress said to Isaiah.

Okay. He's a gentleman.

"Thank you, Isaiah. Although you didn't have to pay."

"Yeah, I know, but I got it."

I glanced down at my watch to see what time it was. I didn't realize how long we had been sitting and talking. It was well into the afternoon and I was still in my workout clothes.

"Wow, I didn't realize how late it was. I am going to head out and get out of these nasty clothes I've been in all morning," I said.

"Thank you, Xenia." Isaiah said.

"For what?" I asked.

"Your company…" he said.

I smiled.

"I'll talk to you later, Isaiah…" I said.

Chapter 21

On my way to work I realized I hadn't spoken with Amy in a while. As I went to pick up my phone, it rang. I thought for a brief moment that it was her until I glanced down at it.

I winced; it was Jake. I hadn't spoken with him since that kiss and now it had been a few weeks. He had called and left messages, but I accidently-on-purpose deleted his messages.

I let it go to voice mail…again. I couldn't talk to him about it, yet. I didn't mean to let him kiss me. I hated I allowed myself to get in that position with him. It was supposed to be an innocent dinner; that's all. Nothing more. Nothing less.

I dialed Amy's number to get my mind off of Jake.

"Hello," she answered.

"Hey, girl, how are ya?" I asked.

"I'm good." She sounded flustered.

"What's wrong?" I asked.

"I'm trying to pack for this trip and I'm trying not to go over the weight limit but I don't think it's working," she said.

"Oh, yes!! The trip is this week. I almost forgot. Well, did you want me to come over after work and help out," I asked.

"Could you, could you?" she said sounding relieved.

"No problem, I'd love to help you for a change," I said laughing.

"Yeah, so, what's good with you this morning? On the way to work?" she asked.

"Yeppers, indeed I am." I replied. I let out a deep sigh.

"Now, what's wrong with you?" she asked.

"What are you talking about?" I responded.

"Why the deep sigh?"

My mind was racing so fast, I hadn't realized I let out a sigh.

"Girl, nothing. So what time did you want me to come by?" I asked.

"You're not coming until you tell me what your deal is!" she said.

"Dang, Amy!!! I am fine," I said.

"Mmmhmm, whatever, chick. Mama knows when something ain't quite right with the milk," she said.

"You sound so old saying that," I said laughing.

"Yeah, I know; now spill it!" she demanded.

There was dead air for a few moments. I realized she wasn't going to let me off the hook.

"Jake and I kissed…" I said, wincing.

"EXCUSE ME!? I knew it was something, but not THAT something!" she exclaimed. How in the world did you let that happen?"

"Trust me when I say it was an accident. Now I'm avoiding his calls," I said.

"When did this happen?" she asked.

"A few weeks ago. I invited him over for dinner, the day of that big presentation at work. After a few glasses of wine, he kissed me and I let him," I said.

"Well, don't go beating yourself up about it. What's done is done. So, is something still there?" she asked.

"Girl…I forgot what it was like to be kissed. It felt good. But, it doesn't mean it was good for me," I said.

"Yeah, I understand that. Well, I'm sure he wants to know what was up with the kiss. You can't avoid him forever Zen," she said.

"I know. When he asks, I'm not going to have an answer for him. I mean not a word," I said.

"Dang girl, I don't have anything for you either. I mean, I wouldn't have guessed you invited him for dinner let alone kissing him," she said. Sounds like you may be on your own with this one."

I laughed and said, "Yeah, sounds like it. There's obviously some unfinished business between the both of us. We had a great time at dinner, the conversation flowed well; it was like old times. Then I clear off the table and I'm at the kitchen sink, turn around and he's right there."

At this point, could my life get any more confusing and complicated? Well, it could, but I'm hoping not.

"Okay, girl, I'm pulling into work, so, I'll see you after I get off."

"Bye, Hun…" Amy said.

I walked into work ready for my workday, trying to put out of my head my encounter with Jake.

I finally looked up at the time and saw that it was after 12 noon. I was starving and I needed to get out of the office to see the light of day and to eat lunch.

I decided to go back to my bar find for something different to eat! As I walked out of my office, I let Sarah know I was going to be out for only a moment and I would be back shortly.

When I walked in, I headed straight for the bar to take my seat. Too bad I couldn't have a drink with lunch. I hadn't really touched much alcohol since the infamous kiss with Jake. The bar tender came over to take my drink order. The only thing I needed was water. While he got my water, I looked over the menu. I placed my food order and, while I waited, I scanned the crowd to see who all was enjoying this place like me.

As I was scanning the crowd, I thought I saw Isaiah sitting at a table towards the back of the bar. In my attempt to be discreet, I looked in his direction again. As my head turned my heart began to race because he or whomever wasn't alone. It was him and he was sitting with a woman.

For some reason, I began to feel some kind of way about it, too!

"Ma'am, here's your Cajun Chicken Pasta dish," the bartender said.

I turned my head quickly like he caught me doing something wrong. Well, I *was* being nosey.

"Thank you so much," I said. I pulled the plate closer to me so I could dig in.

But I couldn't help myself. I had to look again. As I turned my head, they were walking towards the front of the bar to leave. It was him! She was gorgeous—tall, athletic build, gorgeous hair—gorgeous. Then, I looked at Isaiah and we made eye contact.

I smiled and looked back at my food and began to eat. This pasta was amazing! It was so amazing I began to do a little happy dance in my seat. I often did that when the food I was eating was great.

"The food is amazing, right?" the male voice said.

Straight No Chaser: The Beginning

The voice startled me and I looked up to see who it was.

"Hey, Isaiah!" I said with a mouth full of food.

"Hi, Xenia," he said sitting next to me.

"I thought you were leaving," I said.

"I was, and, then, I saw you and I wanted to speak," he said.

"Well, don't keep your date waiting," I said.

Man, why'd I say that? It sounded like I was jealous or something.

Isaiah laughed.

"Xenia. It's not what you're thinking," he said.

"What am I thinking?" I asked him.

Isaiah gave me this look as he flashed those pretty teeth of his and shook his head.

"Alright Ms. Xenia, I'm going to head out. I just wanted to speak before leaving," he said. Hopefully we can link up soon."

I matched his smile and said, "We'll see. Have a good day sir."

As he was walking towards the door to catch up with his lunch date, I glanced at the woman he was with. She was standing waiting for him. As he got closer to her, she glanced at me and raised an eyebrow at me, turned and disappeared behind the door.

Okay, Isaiah, it's not what I think, huh? Yeah, right!

I turned around to finish my pasta so I could hurry back to work.

After work, I almost forgot I told Amy I was going to come by her house. When I remembered, I was almost home. I called her and let her know I was going to change clothes and head over.

When I finally got to her house and walked in, I smelled food!

"YOU cooked!? I can't believe it," I said.

"Yep, courtesy of the Italian spot down the street," she said laughing.

"I should've known better," I said. Either way, it smells great, what did you order?"

"Chicken and shrimp linguine, bread sticks and molten chocolate cake for dessert," she said.

"Whoa, you went all out, didn't you? What's the occasion?" I asked.

"No occasion. I'm just hungry."

Yeah right, Amy wasn't fooling me. She knows I love to eat and she tries to distract me with food when she has something important to say that will more than likely knock me off my feet.

"Okay…" I said as I gave her the side eye.

"No, really it's nothing," she said.

"Well, where are these clothes. It's time for me to show you how to pack for a trip Lucy Pearl," I said laughing.

We walked into the living room and she had clothes and suitcase on her couch. I had my work cut out for me.

"So, all of this is going for sure right?" I asked.

She yelled from the kitchen, "Yep!"

Amy strolled back into the living room chomping on a bread stick. I looked up at her and rolled my eyes.

"What?" she asked.

"Really? You're going to come in here with some bread and not bring me any?" I said. Dang ok. I guess I have to get my own?"

Amy laughed, "Girl, no, I'll get you some bread. Stop your whining."

By the time she came back I had half of her suitcase packed.

"Wait, you're almost done," she asked astonished.

"Uh yeah, it really isn't that hard. You were making things more difficult…as usual." I replied.

She laughed as she placed the bread on the coffee table.

"Anyway, here's your little bread," she said sarcastically.

"You know I'm not going to let it go. What's going on that you're not telling me about?" I asked. I mean, you ordered food; and a lot of it."

Amy was still chomping on the bread and giving me this look. A look I'd never seen before. She had a sparkle in her eyes. There was silence as I was packing her bag and waiting for her to spill the beans.

"We started looking at rings…" she said smiling.

I stopped everything and turned to look at her. My eyes and mouth were wide open!

"SHUT ALL THE WAY UP!" I exclaimed.

Amy looked at me smiling big from ear to ear and nodding her head.

"He didn't even tell me we were going to look. He just drove up to the place one day when we were out. The first weekend we looked, I didn't get too excited. But after the third time, I got really excited!" she explained.

"Oh…my…GOSH girl!!!! I'm so excited for you. Well, there you have it folks. No wonder you ordered food." I said.

"I mean he has turned into somebody I can't see myself living without. I know things may be moving faster than I thought," she said.

I cut her off mid-sentence and said, "When you know, you know. Girl, I don't even want to finish packing this bag. All I want to do now is eat and toast to you guys' happiness."

We both laughed as I started to pack again. But, this time, I packed quicker because I was ready to talk more and eat!

"Alright, I'm done with this bag. All you have to add are your toiletries and you'll be set and ready to go," I said.

We walked into the kitchen to finally eat. My breadstick had already worn off and I was ready for this pasta for the second time in one day!

I looked in the cupboard for wine glasses so we could really enjoy dinner.

I toasted to her and her future and we ate until we were delirious. I didn't even get a chance to tell her about my run in with Isaiah and was fine with that.

Chapter 22

I hadn't worked out in a while so I decided to hit the gym after work. When I walked into the gym, I took a deep breath to take it all in. It was like my second home and it welcomed me back with open arms.

I normally do my own thing when I go to the gym, but I wanted do something more structured. I looked at the class schedule and saw a strength class was going to start in thirty minutes.

I rushed to change my clothes and walked into the studio for class to set up everything I would need. As I started to set up my weights, I felt someone's eyes following me around the room.

After getting to my spot and waiting for the instructor, I scanned the crowd to see who all was there. This was only my third time taking this class and I was inconsistent with my attendance, so my chances of knowing anyone were slim.

My eyes stopped and I saw why I felt eyes on me as I was setting up. I shook my head and smiled. It was Isaiah.

"Well, well, well. What was that you were saying about NOT being a stalker," I asked laughing. I had no idea you were a member here."

"I'm not a stalker and I didn't know you belonged here either," Isaiah said laughing.

Straight No Chaser: The Beginning

"Well, we have a knack for bumping into each other around town, why not add the gym to the ever growing list?" I shaking my head.

The instructor came into the class and started the music.

"Maybe we can catch up after class?" Isaiah asked.

I nodded and did some quick stretches.

Class was actually exactly what I needed. It was challenging, but good. It cleared my head and took away the stress of my work day. Of course, I was a sweaty mess half way through class and by the end of class it was even worse.

Everyone walked out of class a little slower than they walked in, including me.

Isaiah was waiting for me afterwards. We engaged in a little small talk as we walked towards the treadmills. I wanted to get in a short walk before leaving for the evening. Since I was staying over, he walked the treadmill beside me.

I wasn't used to someone talking to me while I worked out. I actually preferred not to talk during workouts, but I guess his company is what I needed because my walk didn't seem to take as long.

We decided to meet in the Café at the gym after getting our things from the locker room. I was starving of course, so I couldn't wait to get there!

I sat my things down where he was sitting and I plopped down in my seat, exhausted.

Isaiah looked at me and said, "Tired?"

I glared at him and said, "DUDE!!! She tried to kill us!"

He laughed.

"Yeah, she's a tough cookie, but I like her class. By looking at her, you wouldn't think she's as strong as she is," he said.

"Yeah. Okay, I'm hungry. I'm going to order my food," I said.

"Wait up, I'm ordering too!" he said, following me.

We ordered our food and, surprisingly, he paid for us both again. I wasn't expecting him to pay. We sat back down and waited for our order to be prepared.

It took the staff ten minutes to get our food out to us. I was about to enjoy my *bar-b-que* pizza I ordered and a salad. The salad looked amazing. The best part about this place was their dressing! It's the little things that make me smile.

Isaiah stared at me until I broke the silence.

"What is it?" I asked.

"Even after your workout, you're beautiful," he said.

"Is that a compliment?" I asked laughing.

Straight No Chaser: The Beginning

"Yeah, it is. I'm sorry, I didn't mean it the way it obviously sounded," he said.

"Well, let me bask in my after-workout glow," I said.

After finishing up our dinner, we sat and just enjoyed each other's company. By this time I wasn't feeling antsy at all. I didn't feel nervous like I normally did. Is this what it feels like to let loose a little? It had been a while since I had just gotten to know someone like this. I guess I had built a wall taller than I realized.

In the middle of our conversation, Isaiah glanced over at the door, which made me glance down at my watch to see what time it was.

"Oh, man, I didn't realize the time," I said.

I noticed he was a little figgity.

"Umm, are you alright?" I asked.

"Yep, I am," Isaiah said.

He kept glancing at the door, so I turned around to see what or who he was looking at. It was the gorgeous woman he was with at lunch a few days prior.

"Listen, why don't you go speak to your friend. I won't keep you any longer than I already have. I do have a busy day to get ready for tomorrow," I said.

"Oh, umm, well, I guess…" he said.

Straight No Chaser: The Beginning

Although I knew it then, I knew there was something more with those two than he tried to let on. I don't know who he thought he was fooling.

I laughed and shook my head as I was getting up.

"Hi, Zay…" a female voice said.

"Heeeyyy, how are you?" Isaiah said, nervously.

The woman hugged Isaiah kind of tightly. After she let him go, she turned and smiled at me while taking a step closer to Isaiah.

"Hi…" she said.

I matched her smile and said, "Hi, how are you?"

"Oh, I'm great now that I'm seeing this face," she said, referring to Isaiah.

"Great! Well, you two have a good evening. Isaiah, thanks again for dinner," I said.

As I turned to walk away, I felt the mystery woman's eyes pierce the back of my head. This situation should have been weird for me, but it wasn't.

By the time I reached my car, my text message alert was going off. After settling in the car, I looked at my phone.

Xenia, I'm sorry about that. I should've introduced you. I don't know what I was thinking.

Surprisingly, I replied back to Isaiah.

No worries. It may good you didn't I don't need to add her to my list of stalkers LOL

He didn't respond.

Chapter 23

I had been assigned another major project that I had been working on for about a month. This particular project was more tedious and worth more money to the company. So, it was imperative that I concentrate more than usual.

This also meant my working like crazy again and my social life taking another hit. I hadn't really spoken with anyone or hung out. It was starting to take a toll on me, but I wouldn't change it for the world! I was enjoying my job and my new position.

When I was assigned the project, I wondered if Isaiah would be on the legal side of things, again. I guess the Team doesn't know until the firm assigns the lawyers. Since it wasn't time to bring them in, I didn't bring it up to my team.

I decided to work remotely over the weekend. I searched the internet all week for different restaurants I could bunker down and put in some major hours. I have it kind of bad for food.

Before I bunkered down, I decided to take Friday night for myself and treat myself to dinner and a movie.

After the long and stressful week I had, I decided to stop by the bar right after work, to get my party started. Before walking in, I decided to only have one drink.

I walked into the bar and headed straight to my favorite bar tender. He saw me coming and smiled.

Straight No Chaser: The Beginning

"Well, hello there, stranger," he said.

"Hey, Mike!! I missed you!" I said.

"I missed you, too, pretty lady,." Mike said. Your usual?"

I laughed and said, "You know it!"

I settled into my seat and Mike slid the glass of whiskey in front of me.

"There you go. What's been going on since I hadn't seen you in awhile?" he asked.

"Not much, man, just working. Oh, I did get a promotion at work," I said.

"Oooh, so, that's why I hadn't seen you?" Mike said.

"Yep, paying my dues. But, I'm definitely not complaining about it. It's actually better than I thought it would be," I said.

"Good deal and congratulations to you. Did you want to look at a menu or are you going to get your usual?" he asked.

"Ya know, I hadn't even thought about food, BUT, I will try your spinach dip this time and, instead of chips, can I get the bread with it?" I asked.

"Coming right up!" he said. He walked away to put my order in.

It was only fifteen minutes after five and the bar was full of stressed out people who may have had the same week I had at work. I smiled as I scanned the crowd and I took a sip of my drink. Mike brought the spinach dip and bread out to me and I did my happy dance because I was starving. I hadn't eaten anything since lunch.

Since I decided on dinner and a movie I went ahead and ordered dinner as well. Since it was so good the last time, I ordered the *Duck Confit* again.

By the time I ordered dinner the bar was packed to capacity and they had a pretty long wait time. Glad I got there when I did.

My Duck came out and looked amazing and I couldn't wait to tear into it. Just as soon as I picked up my utensils I felt a tap on my shoulder. Given the history of our run-ins, I knew exactly who it was.

I turned around and said, "Well, well, well…so, we meet again?" My face dropped immediately.

"Hi, Zen." Jake said. "What's wrong!?"

"Umm, nothing," I said. I just knew it was Isaiah. How are you?"

"I'm good. I'm meeting a friend for dinner and on the way to our table I saw you and wanted to say hi," he said.

"You're on a date?" I asked.

"Yeah…I am," he said reluctantly.

"Cool, well, I hope you guys have a good time," I said.

Straight No Chaser: The Beginning

Jake smiled and walked over to his date. From what I saw she was pretty. I felt a little jealous. Maybe it was because I was there alone. But, at least I didn't look like a raga-muffin! So, I felt a little better about that.

"Hey, beautiful, how's everything?" Mike asked.

I mustered up a smile and said, "Yeah, the Duck is amazing and the spinach dip, oh my God, the best I've had in a while."

"Awesome," Mike said. He walked away to check on the other patrons at the bar.

I took another sip of my drink and bite of my duck. When I glanced up I noticed someone looking at me. When I took a closer look, it was Isaiah.

He smiled. I smiled and I tipped my glass to him. Of course, there was an empty seat next to me. It seemed like he was in the seat in 2 seconds flat.

"The prettiest thing at the bar, I had to come sit beside you," Isaiah said.

I smirked and shook my head.

"What? You like shaking your head at me…" he said.

"Nothing. Nice of us to run into each other…again." I said.

He let out a big laugh.

"We have to stop running into each other like this. Why don't you let me take you out one night?" Isaiah said.

Straight No Chaser: The Beginning

I was actually thinking about it.

"Why should I after you stood me up the last time?" I asked. I took another sip of my drink.

"You're right and I tried explaining what happened, but you weren't trying to hear it," he said.

"You're right, I wasn't," I said taking another sip. I motioned for Mike to make another drink.

"How many of those have you had?" he asked.

"Two. Thanks Mike."

"What are you drinking, my man?" Mike said.

"I'll have a Scotch on the rocks," Isaiah said.

Mike walked away to fix Isaiah's drink.

"So, what do you say, Xenia?" he asked.

"I'll think about it," I said.

I looked at Isaiah and smiled. He matched my smile.

"Well, we're getting closer to a yes," he said sipping his Scotch.

Isaiah looked over his menu for this dinner choices while I was still working on my dinner.

"So, where's your friend this evening?" I asked.

"Here we go. I told you she's just a friend," he said.

"A friend who made it very clear that she wanted to be more when we met," I said.

"Yeah, I talked to her about that," he said.

I looked at him and raised my brow.

"Okay, well moving on. How are you?" I asked. How was the week?"

"No way, we aren't talking about work tonight. I have to work all weekend. Tonight, I clear my head," he said.

Mike brought Isaiah's food and we toasted to a night of letting our hair down.

"Your food looks good," I said.

"Did you want to try it?" he asked.

"Nah, I try not to eat off people's plates because I don't want them eating off of mine," I said.

We talked into the evening. The movie I wanted to see, I missed. It was too late for me to go now. Besides, I think I was on the verge of being drunk; I was on my fourth whiskey. I excused myself to the restroom to get myself together because I realized I was indeed drunk!

When I came back to my seat, I found out Isaiah had paid our dinner bills.

"Hey, there you go, you okay?" he asked.

"Yes, I'm fine," I said as I sat down.

"You want to get dessert?" he asked.

"I could go for ice cream," I said.

"Well, since you've been drinking, I'm driving and I can drop you off at home," he said.

"No, I think I can manage," I said. I knew I shouldn't drive, but I didn't want to be around him alone in close quarters either.

"Xenia, yeah okay, let's go," he demanded.

We pulled up to the ice cream parlor and walked inside. I was like a kid in a candy store. I lit up as soon as I walked in.

We ordered and sat at the table in the front window. Although inebriated, I was enjoying Isaiah's company. Our conversation flowed.

After we finished our sweet treats, he drove me home. We pulled into the driveway and I had butterflies in my stomach. I felt like I was in high school on my first date.

"So, here we are," I said.

"Let me walk you to the door."

"Oh, you don't have to do that."

"Let me be a gentleman, please?" he said.

He got out of the car and opened my door. When we got to my front door I put the key in the door. I turned around to tell him good night.

Straight No Chaser: The Beginning

"Well, thanks for a nice evening Isaiah. You're an okay dude," I said smiling. "Thanks for driving me home."

"I enjoyed you as well and no problem. I was not going to let you drive your self home," he said.

Our eyes connected and I felt a strong, electric force between us. Then he stroked my cheek lightly. I took a step closer to the door. He matched my step.

"Well…" I said clearing my throat. I have to get inside, I have a big day tomorrow."

"Xenia, you are so beautiful. Even if you are drunk," he said.

We both burst out laughing. After a few seconds of laughter and we looked at each other again. I kissed Isaiah. At least I think I did. Maybe we leaned in at the same time.

While we were kissing, I opened the door to stop us. This kiss was hot and got me more bothered than I wanted to be at the moment.

He followed me inside, never stopping his kiss.

I didn't want him to stop. So, I just 'let go.' I couldn't help it and I didn't want to. I don't know what it was, but he kissed me so passionately. I felt so beautiful. Maybe it was the alcohol.

He pressed me against the door after closing it. He intertwined his fingers with mine and raised my arms on the door. It was so sexy. He reached down and rubbed my leg and began to pull up my skirt. At that moment, I snapped back to reality, opened my eyes and quickly stopped him.

"Gosh, umm, we gotta stop. This is going way too fast. I can't do this, Isaiah," I said, quickly.

"I'm sorry, I don't know what came over me," he said.

"I'm not completely innocent here," I said. Thanks for the ride home, I'll get my car later. Have a good night."

I pushed him out the door. When the door slammed, I fell on the door and slid down to the floor. I couldn't believe what had just happened. I headed to my room to shower and called it a night because, clearly, I wasn't in my right mind.

Chapter 24

Dear God,

Please guide my footsteps and help me to make the right decisions in my life because, clearly, I should not be left unattended.

I sat on my bed just thinking over my life, especially the past few months or so and I almost felt like my personal life was a recipe for disaster. I needed to get it together and quick!

Jake's kiss made me realize how long it had actually been since I had kissed someone. Isaiah's kiss reminded me of how long it had been since—well, you know.

I couldn't handle all of this. I was not emotionally stable enough to handle this. I'm trying not to make any rushed decisions, but it was becoming too much. I really couldn't talk to anyone about it right now. Not until I could actually put what and how I was feeling into words.

This was going to be another weekend of getting work done. Before starting on my project, I wanted to go for a run to clear my head before working.

Me and Isaiah's kiss was still fresh on my mind. I couldn't shake it and it had been almost two weeks! This guy would not leave my head no matter what I tried. I couldn't concentrate on anything that needed my undivided attention.

Straight No Chaser: The Beginning

After hitting the pavement, two miles in, I had a flashback of me and Isaiah. I shook my head, like that was really going to help. After the third flashback, I stopped my run. I found a bench to stretch my legs and to get it together. My run was not working in my favor today. While I was sitting down, I watched the other runners in the park, I watched the families out spending time together and I smiled.

I smiled because it gave me hope that one day I'd be at the park with my family spending quality time together.

I got up to walk around the park before heading back home. I walked over to the pond and when I got there I was one of the few gathered there. Some of the smaller kids were chasing one another and the ducks.

Eventually, I ran back home to shower and get my day started.

Later that day I was sitting in the kitchen working on my project, when I heard the doorbell. Another unexpected guest? I continued to work. The doorbell rang again, this time twice in a row.

I got up to see who it was. I looked out the peep hole to see who it was. Surprise, surprise. I opened the door.

"Hey Zen," Isaiah said.

"Calling me Zen, now?" I asked.

"Yeah, I kinda figured after the other night, I could call you that now," he said smiling.

I didn't find it too amusing.

"So, you couldn't call first?" I asked.

"I was afraid you wouldn't answer," he said.

He was probably right. I wanted to slam the door in his face, but then again I wanted him to kiss me again.

"You want to come in, no need to keep you standing out here," I said.

He came inside and sat down on the couch. I was still standing. I refused to sit on the same couch as him. He smelled amazing.

"So, what are you up to today?" he asked.

"Work. I'm up to my eyeballs in it," I said. "I can't wait until this project is over with!"

"Another project? That's a good look. Your bosses must have been impressed last time," he said.

"Yep. They were," I said.

There was dead air. We just looked at each other.

"Zen are you going to have a seat?" he asked.

"No, I'm good," I said.

"You can't just stand up the entire time," he said.

"And just how long do you plan on being here?" I asked laughing.

"Not long…" he said laughing. You kicking me out already?"

"No, it's not that, I mean you did show up unannounced," I said.

"Okay, let me get to the point then. The other night, I had the time of my life with you. The kiss was something I'd never experienced before. The spark was something else," he said.

"Just the kiss?" I asked.

"No, the entire night was amazing," he said.

"That night was great. The kiss was pretty darn good, to the point it scared me," I said.

I finally sat on the couch, but on the opposite end.

"I don't want anything to scare you when you're with me," he said.

"I just got out of a relationship a while back and I'm trying to get over it still, and adding you to the mix confuses things," I explained.

"I understand." he said. The thing is, I still want to get to know you. I know my separation gives you pause, but is there something wrong with us being friends," he asked.

"No, it's not, but what kind of friends are you talking about," I asked. With benefits or without?"

He smirked.

Straight No Chaser: The Beginning

"Zen, we're both adults and I think we can handle whatever this turns into," he said.

This guy thinks he's slick! He just said he wanted to be friends with benefits without saying it. I almost forgot he's a lawyer and can get crafty with his words.

"You're funny. So you want to be friends with benefits, huh?" I asked.

"I didn't say that, Zen."

I smiled and shook my head.

"You didn't have to say it."

At that moment I decided to let go a little.

"So, what now?" I said.

"Not sure, whatever we want," he said.

This was playing out too much like a movie. He got up from his side of the couch to sit next to me. I felt myself getting nervous and I repositioned myself on the couch. He leaned in to kiss me. I stayed in my same position not moving until I felt him pull me closer to him.

He kissed me passionately. I tried pulling away until I got tired of fighting it and then I melted into his arms. He picked me up and sat me on his lap. This could not go any further than this kiss. But my body was definitely saying otherwise. He began to rub my back under my shirt. I pulled his hand free from under my shirt. I will not do this...I will not do this.

Straight No Chaser: The Beginning

"Isaiah, we have to stop," I said flustered.

I knew it. I showed my hand way to soon and now I can't stop these feelings. I leaped off his lap.

"You need to go, Isaiah. I have a lot of work to do today," I said, walking towards the door.

"I'm sorry, Zen. I can't help it when I'm around you I...," he said.

I cut him off mid-sentence.

"Don't apologize, just...you have to go." I said. This can not happen."

He got up from the couch to leave. He looked good standing there in his sweats. I went to open the door and our hands touched. There was that magnetic energy again. I looked at him and he looked at me. He took me into his arms, again, and kissed me.

Okay, that was it, I couldn't hold back any longer.

I rolled over in the bed and looked at the ceiling. I couldn't believe what had just happened. I know I said 'let go, let flow' but I wasn't planning to let go *like this*! I will say, it was amazing. This man took his time and made every inch of me feel beautiful.

I looked over at him, while he was napping and smiled. I got up from bed and headed into the bathroom on a high. It seemed like I was floating on air. When I came back out Isaiah was awake.

"Well, sir, did you have a good nap?" I asked.

"I did," he said smiling. Hey, listen, you want to get dinner later?"

"I'd love to but I'm behind on work for some reason," I said, clearing my throat.

He laughed.

"Well, maybe I can drop something by for you later," he asked.

"That's sweet, Isaiah," I said blushing. "I'll let you know."

Isaiah got himself together and left.

After he left, I got myself together and got back to work.

What did I just do? It hit me!

I just slept with a married man!!!!

Chapter 25

"**Amy**, hey it's Zen. I finally wrapped up the project at work and now back in the land of the living. When you get this, call me, babes."

I hadn't spoken to hardly anyone since I started working on this project. Believe you me, I was glad that it was over and done with.

I felt like celebrating and, since Amy wasn't answering her phone, I went through my phone to see who I wanted in my space for a few hours.

Everyone I called was busy so I guess it was all me tonight. I ordered pizza and decided to have wine as well. I checked my fridge to see what I had. I saw I was out of my favorite Chatham Hill wine so I called in my pizza order, threw on my sweats so I could pick up the wine and pizza.

I ran into the grocery store first for the wine and picked up chips and salsa, too. On my way out, I ran into Isaiah and his lady friend. The same lady friend he said meant nothing to him.

"Hi guys, how's it going?" I asked.

No wonder he didn't answer when I called earlier.

"Hi there, we're good," Isaiah said. "Just picking up some things for dinner."

"Great, well you guys have a great evening," I said as I rushed to my car.

Straight No Chaser: The Beginning

His friend never said anything. Before going home, I swung by to pick up the pizza and rushed home to have a party by myself. After I got back home and settled in, I was almost glad no one answered their phone.

As soon as I sat down, my doorbell rang. This time I knew who it wasn't. I looked through the peephole; it was Jake this time. What is going on that everyone wants to come by here unannounced?

I opened the door.

"Hi Jake."

"Hey, Zen. I know, I'm sorry," he said. "But I did see you called earlier. I dropped by because I was in the area."

"Do better," I said laughing. "Come in. I called because I wrapped up my project this week."

"Good for you. You worked on that one for a long time, I know you're glad," he said.

"Yes, beyond glad. Tonight, I celebrate." I said.

"We got pizza and Chatham Hill? Okayyyy," Jake said. "What are you watching?"

"Not sure yet, still trying to decided," I said.

My phone interrupted me.

"Excuse me for a second," I said.

I walked over to my cell to see who it was. Isaiah. Now, why is he calling me? I thought he was having dinner with his friend? I sent him to voice mail. I turned to go back to the couch and my phone rang again. I sent Isaiah to voice mail again.

"I didn't interrupt anything, did I?" Jake asked.

"What do you mean?" I asked.

"You weren't expecting anyone, were you?" he asked.

"Oh, no, not this time," I said.

"Listen, I know you saw me out on a date a while back," he said. I just wanted to make sure things were okay between me and you."

I was a tad bit confused.

"Between me and you? What are you talking about," I asked.

"The kiss, and then you saw me out with another woman," he explained.

"Jake, dear heart. We aren't together anymore. Meaning, we both can do whatever we want right?" I asked.

Jake had this look on his face like he wasn't expecting me to say that.

"Well, I guess. Yeah, you're right," he said.

"Is that the only reason you came by here? Jake you've obviously been doing whatever you want for a while; we hadn't been together in months. Did you think I'd be upset?" I asked.

"Umm, well nah, I didn't think that," he said.

"Okay, cool. We kissed one night after drinking, that was it. I will say at that moment it felt like old times, but we can't go back to where we were," I said. "If we did, it wouldn't be now. I'm not over your cheating."

Jake sat quietly for a moment.

"Understood. So, what do I have to do?" he asked.

"Do?" I asked. I was really confused now.

"To get you back in my life?" he said.

I was not expecting that.

"Jake, I can't with this conversation right now. My pizza is getting cold and I'm starving," I said.

I know I called him earlier to hang, but if he's trying to talk about getting back together then he's got to GO!

"I'll call you later, okay?" I told him.

He looked so sad. But, I knew this game and I refused to fall for it tonight. So, I stood up and walked towards the door. He followed suit, thank goodness.

"Zen, I still love you. See ya," he said walking out of the house.

I completely froze when he said that. I closed the door behind him and grabbed a slice of pizza as I plopped on the couch. I completely ignored what he said.

Straight No Chaser: The Beginning

Did I still love him? Yes, I did. Why couldn't he do this when we were together? He's working harder to get me back than he was to keep me! What sense did that make? NONE!

I decided on watching an Independent film on Netflix. An hour or so into the film, my doorbell rang—again. I knew this couldn't be Jake coming back! I got up to see who it was through the peephole.

I smiled at who it was as I opened the door.

"Hey, girl, I'm so glad it's you. Get in here we need to catch up!" I exclaimed.

I hadn't seen Amy in forever and I was glad she stopped by.

"Girl, I got your message earlier and since I was in the area, decided to stop by. I brought a bottle of wine for your collection, but I see you already cracked a bottle open," she said laughing.

"I could always use another bottle," I told her.

I sat the bottle on the coffee table as we sat on the couch.

"Okay, so, what's been up girl?" Amy asked. I know we hadn't really talked because of this project you were working on."

"Other than that, that's all I could do! Jake just left here about an hour ago," I told her.

Straight No Chaser: The Beginning

Amy was fixing her a glass of wine from the bottle I had opened and stopped pouring when I said Jake's name.

"And why did he just leave here?" she asked slowly.

"Girl, please! No!! He stopped by to talk about getting back together," I replied.

"Back together? He's working overtime to get you back, huh?" Amy said laughing.

"Yes girl! It's flattering and everything, but why is he working so hard now? When we were together, he didn't work half as hard to keep me."

"Well, Zen, I know you don't want to hear this, but I think you should hear him out. You never know," she said. I mean the night he kissed you, you even said that the night was perfect, the conversation flowed and it felt like old times."

I didn't say anything after she said that.

"Hello, is anyone there?" Amy asked, sarcastically. You don't have to tell me I'm right. I'll take your silence to mean just that."

We both burst out laughing.

"Girl, whatever. Why can't they just get it right the first time? Men are always talking about finding and getting a good girl and when they get one, they don't know what to do with her. I'm tired. You know how many guys I dated before we finally hooked up that took me through that same thing?" I said.

Straight No Chaser: The Beginning

"Yeah, I know. We both have that track record. But, you have to keep the faith that the right one will be worth all the frustrations and heartache," she said.

"Yeah, he better be worth it, because I am tired of this entire dating game thing," I said.

I was thinking about telling Amy what happened between me and Isaiah, but I was scared! I think she read my facial expression.

"Okay, I've been trying to ignore it and be patient. What's wrong? What's on your mind?" she asked. I can tell something is on your mind so don't try saying nothing."

Dang it. I gotta work on my facial expressions. I mean, I wanted to talk to her about it. But, then again, I didn't. I guess I was scared of being judged and didn't want her to fuss me out for falling. I blurted it out.

"I slept with Isaiah…" I said.

Amy looked at me with a blank stare and didn't say a word. I looked at her and scrunched my lips to one side.

"I know…you don't even have to say anything!" I said.

Amy cut me off mid-sentence.

"I know you didn't just tell me you spent the night with a married man; separated or whatever he is!?. Girl, are you out of your mind!? What is going on with you?" she screamed.

"See, this is why I didn't want to tell you," I said. I already feel bad enough without you yelling at me."

I really did feel bad. I worked so hard to stay away from this guy and not let my guard down, then bam! I let my guard down and what did I do? Ugh!

"Well, I'm sorry. But, what happened to the plan you told me about? Staying away from him and not putting yourself in that position," she asked.

"Hold up, Lucy Pearl. It was YOU that said, on more than one occasion, might I add, *you never know he could be the one; let your guard down; stop being so hard on men*," I reminded her.

Amy had a look on her face like 'oh yeah, I did say that.'

"Okay. I'm sorry, but I didn't think you'd spend the night with the man, girl," she said. "Look, sorry for yelling."

"I feel bad enough about it. But, he obviously caught me at a vulnerable moment. It's like the envelope was closed, but he kept prying at it and when he pried it open just enough, you know the rest," I said.

"Ok, well, we're not going to beat ourselves up over it. We'll rebound from this and keep things moving forward. No more Isaiah. Right?" she asked.

"I'm not planning on anything else happening. I just need to work overtime now for it not to happen. Meaning, try and avoid him at all costs," I said.

"Well, I didn't ask. But, how did this come about anyway?" she asked.

I completely forgot to give her the back story.

"Yeah, I didn't tell you that, did I? Well, one Friday after work, I went to Happy Hour at this bar by myself and he happened to be there and I had one too many whiskey's and was in no condition to drive. So, after dinner, we went for ice cream and he drove me home. He walked me to the door and we kissed. Nothing happened that night. Fast-forward, a couple of weeks later, one Saturday afternoon, I was here working on the project and he stopped by. We were talking and the next thing I know…well, you know," I explained.

"Wow. Well, I gotta ask. Was it worth it?" she asked.

I smiled and nodded my head.

"Girl, it was pretty darn good," I said. But, he's married and I can't go down this road with him or anyone else for that matter. I feel like the poster girl for sluts-are-us!" I said.

Amy laughed.

"Girl, I'm serious. Ugh," I said. How could I let this happen? I shouldn't be left unattended right now."

"Well, like I said, don't beat yourself up about it. He caught you on an off day. Just don't let it happen again," she said sternly.

Straight No Chaser: The Beginning

"You don't have to worry about that one," I told her. Okay, enough about my crazy past couple of weeks. Let's talk about this trip you went on! I want to know everything."

Amy was grinning from ear to ear.

"Girl, this was the best trip of my LIFE!" she exclaimed. The first couple of days we were there, we stayed in the room the entire day, ordered room service, drank and watched movies all day. It was lovely. I didn't realize how tired I actually was. The rest of the time we were there, we laid on the beach, went zip-lining one day, walked on the beach at sunset. And…we had a picnic on the beach one night," she said smiling.

"Why would you have a picnic at night?" I asked.

Amy tilted her head and gave me her famous blank stare.

"Why are you looking at me like tha…ooooh, you had a 'picnic' I get it now!" I said laughing at myself.

"You are so slow sometimes, I swear!" Amy said shaking her head at me and laughing.

I looked down and saw we devoured the pizza and wine. I got up to open the bottle she brought over. I was still hungry.

I yelled from the kitchen, "Hey, do you want chips and salsa!?"

"Sure! Bring it on!" Amy said. Grab another bottle of wine while you're in there!"

I grabbed everything in my arms and came back out to the living room.

"You need some help?" Amy asked.

"Nope, I got it, BUT you can take the wine." I told her. So has there been any more marriage talk? Please don't tell me you got married while you were there."

"Girl, no! I would've led with that news! We are still looking at rings, and I'm trying to stay cool," she said.

"I am so excited for you, girl. What do your parents think about him?" I asked.

"They love him! My dad especially loves him because he's a hard worker. My mom loves him because he's so handsome and treats me like a man should," Amy said.

"Even better when the parentals love him," I said. So whenever I get a consistent man in my life maybe we can double date."

"That would be great. I don't think you've seen him since that night we first met," she said.

"Nope. Sure haven't. Just so he treats you well, which sounds like he is, he's good in my book," I said.

"Awe, thanks girl,…that means a lot to me. He really is God-sent. Just when I was about to give up, he came into my life," she said.

As Amy was talking about her man, I couldn't help but think and ask myself—when was it going to be my turn for the happiness she was experiencing? I couldn't wait, but I didn't want to rush it, either.

"Girl, you do know you're not going home tonight, right?" I asked Amy.

"Why not," she asked.

"This is our second bottle. I'm not letting you drive home, so you can park it in the guest room tonight. Thanks," I said.

Amy looked at the bottles and thought for a second.

"Yeah, well, I guess you're right," she said laughing.

"That just means we can do brunch tomorrow," I said.

Any excuse for me to eat!

"Deal…" she said.

We talked into the night. When we were tired of talking we watched a movie and eventually drifted off to sleep on the couch. This was a night well-spent.

Chapter 26

I slid against the wall, down to the floor. I couldn't believe it. As I sat on the floor, I felt a tear roll down my cheek. I sat there for, I know, three hours; or it felt like three hours. I couldn't move…like, at all!

After denying it for three months, there I was on the floor in my bathroom holding a pregnancy test. I took the test four different times, and they all said the same thing.

"Positive," I whispered to myself. This has got to be wrong! I can't be pregnant. Not now. Hell, not ever!!"

I mustered up strength from somewhere, got off the floor and walked into my bedroom and sat on the bed. I still had the test in my hands. When I sat down I took a deep breath and slowly let it out. I began to cry—uncontrollably.

I could not believe this. This is what going with the flow gets you…in trouble! Oh, my gosh, now I have to call Isaiah and tell him. It had been a week since we'd seen each other and I had just spoken with him last night. I cannot believe this!

I went to pick up the phone to call Amy, but I couldn't find it in me to dial her number. I put my phone down. I needed to call Isaiah, but I knew he was working on a project for work and was busy.

Okay, Zen, now you're just making excuses not to call and let him know. Yes, he's separated from his wife, but he's still married with his own kids with her! This is a dream. I know it. I sat on my bed honestly waiting to wake up from this nightmare. Sounds crazy, I know, but I couldn't be reading this test correctly!

POSITIVE!!! As in, you're going to be a mama in six months!

"I'm not ready to be anybody's mother!" I said out loud.

I fell back on the bed and screamed. I stopped because I didn't want my neighbors thinking I was being attacked. I sat back up on the bed and walked into the kitchen. I was looking for alcohol and I needed something hard. This information deserved a glass of whiskey.

I carried the bottle with me as I sat at the kitchen table. I sat in the dark contemplating on what to do and how to digest this news I didn't want to read on that stick.

Should I keep it? Should I keep it and give the baby up for adoption? Should I get rid of it? My head was swirling and I started crying, again. I'm a single woman, with no man and I'm pregnant. Good going, Zen!

It had been about 3 months so, whatever I decided, I needed to decide, like today.

Isaiah needed to know, but how would I tell him this. This was just supposed to be something casual every now and again. No strings attached. Well, this string is going to be attached for the next 18 years!!! Oh, Lord!

Everybody's going to flip when I tell them the news if I decide to keep it. I'm an adult, yes, but mama is going to kill me. This is not how I pictured my life, having my family live in different households.

I left work early today because my head was killing me. How am I going to act when I get back tomorrow? Oh my goodness, is my being pregnant going to affect my job? I just got this promotion!

I poured more whiskey in the glass, then I realized—I CAN'T DRINK!!! I got up from the table and poured what was in my glass down the drain. See, I don't need a kid forgetting simple stuff like that!

I looked at my cell phone again and picked it up to call Amy.

"Amy, hey, girl. I need you to come over. NOW." I demanded. I didn't wait for a response, I hung up on her.

I don't know what I interrupted, but it seemed like she was at my house three seconds after we got off the phone. As I was walking into the living room, the doorbell rang.

"What is so important I had to rush over here? Are you okay?" she asked.

I showed her the pregnancy test that was in my hand. Amy looked at it and saw that it read positive. There was a few moments of dead air. She walked over to the couch and plopped down.

"Sweetie. Are you okay? Come sit down." she said.

"Want a drink? Because I'm not supposed to," I said.

"Zen, baby, I'll get it. Yes, where's that whiskey?" she yelled as she walked into the kitchen.

"It's on the kitchen table," I said.

"Were you drinking this?" she asked.

"Yep, then I realized. I can't drink so I poured it down the drain," I said.

"Okay. How long have you known?" she asked.

"Thirty minutes ago," I said with tears in my eyes.

Amy hugged me tight. I loved her hugs. It was just what I needed.

"Amy, I can't have this baby! I'm not old enough yet. I don't have all of my stuff together. I can hardly take care of myself, now I'm carrying a little life that will depend on me for everything. I can't do this," I said.

Amy let me get everything out. I'm not sure how she understood what I said through all of my crying and snotting all over her lap. She's a good friend.

"Lucy Pearl, are you finished?" she asked and started laughing.

That was my nickname for her. I'm glad she was trying to make me laugh, because I needed it.

"It's Isaiah's?" she asked.

I looked at her shocked.

"Girl, you know I don't do anything casual like that with everybody. Yes, it's his. He's the only person I've been with since me and Jake broke up." I replied.

"Does he know yet?" she asked.

"Not yet," I said.

"Well, do you plan on telling him?" she asked.

I paused. Evidently, longer than she wanted me to pause.

"Miss girl, when are you planning on telling him!?" she yelled.

"I'm going to tell him! Can I freak out first, digest this information, THEN tell him? I know he's going to freak out. But, do I have to tell him if I decide not to keep it?" I asked.

Amy cut her eye at me.

"Alright! I'll tell him, regardless."

"What do you mean regardless? Regardless of what?" she said.

"IF I keep the baby."

"Zen," she gasped. She looked so hurt when I said that.

"I'm sorry Amy. I never thought I'd be in this situation. Please forgive me!! I'm scared to death! I just found out I'm pregnant by a man I'm not even in a relationship with!" I yelled.

"Okay, okay. Let us both calm down," she said. "I don't even know what to say. I'm speechless."

"Yep, me too. Well, I need to call my doctor and make an appointment just to make sure it's 100% true, that I'm pregnant," I said reluctantly.

Amy and I sat in the living room talking and sitting in silence. We sat a majority of the time in silence. I couldn't cry any more.

I glanced at the time and saw it was 8:00 pm. Amy looked at her cell phone as well.

"Oh, gosh! I forgot I was supposed to meet David for dinner tonight," she said.

"Girl, go be with your man. I've held you up long enough. Thanks for dropping everything to be with me. I'm sorry for being so needy." I said.

"Girl, no worries. We all have our days," she said.

"Yeah, well, I guess I'll be needy for the next six months. Thanks again," I said.

I walked her to the door and she hugged me again before leaving.

I walked back over to the couch. As soon as I plopped down, my phone rang. I glanced down to see who it was. I was prepared to send whomever to voice mail. Then my heart stopped. It was Isaiah.

Before I thought about it, I answered the phone.

"Hello?" I said

"Hey how are you?" he asked.

"Umm, I'm okay. How are you?" I asked.

"I'm doing great now that I hear your voice. I called you at work today, but Sarah said you left early. You sick?" he asked.

"Yeah, something like that," I responded.

"You don't sound like yourself, you want me to come over?" he asked.

"No, no I've actually been in bed since I got home. I may be contagious and I don't want to get you sick," I said.

"Oh okay" he said. He sounded like he didn't believe a word I just told him.

"Okay, well, I'll let you get some rest, pretty lady."

"Okay. Oh, and thanks for checking on me," I said.

I picked up the remote to surf through the channels. Nothing was on that would keep my mind off my news. Then my doorbell rang.

"You have got to be kidding me," I said out loud.

I looked through the peephole. I opened the door.

"Isaiah, can you please stop coming by without calling first?" I demanded.

"Technically, I did call," he said smiling. But, I didn't believe you when you said nothing was wrong and it appears I was right."

"Yeah, but I'm fine," I told him.

"Are you going to invite me in?" he asked.

I opened the door a little wider so he could pass me. He headed over to the couch.

"Would you like something to drink?" I asked.

"Nah, I'm good. I told you I came to check on you," he said.

I forgot I had the test on the coffee table and my heart began to race. My eyes began to wonder around the room.

"What is wrong with you tonight?" he asked.

"Nothing," I said. I still don't feel that great."

"Okay," he said.

There was a moment of silence.

"Zen, what is this?" I heard Isaiah ask.

"What's what?" I replied.

What I didn't want to happen, happened. He did see the test and I was not ready to have this conversation with him.

When I looked at him he was pointing at the test on the coffee table. I closed my eyes and opened them again.

"Um so about that. I'm pregnant," I said reluctantly.

I felt my eyes fill with water. He was silent. He sat there looking at the test.

"How? I mean, I know how, but we were careful?" he said.

"Obviously, not that careful. I thought you had strapped up?" I asked.

"Yeah, I did."

"Well, it must have broken or something," I said.

"When did you notice you were late?" he asked.

"I don't know, sometime last month? I've been so stressed with work I lost track," I explained.

"Okay, so, you're sure the baby's mine?" he asked.

"Dude, I can't believe you're asking me this? I don't hop beds. I can't believe you're asking me this!" I yelled. But, to ease YOUR mind, YES, it's yours."

He didn't say anything; he collapsed back on the couch and covered his eyes with his hands.

"This is not good. This is not good," He kept repeating to himself.

"Yeah, well, I agree," I said.

"So, what are you going to do?" he asked.

My eyes pierced him. I felt myself getting more and more upset.

"What do you mean, what am I going to do? This is our decision. So what, you want to me to get rid of it or something?" I asked.

He looked at me silently.

"Get out! Get out now!" I demanded.

Isaiah got up and walked towards the door.

"Zen, I…" he said.

I cut him off mid-sentence because I didn't want to hear anything he had to say at this point.

"I don't want to hear it! Get out!! NOW!" I yelled.

I slammed the door behind him.

I cried myself to sleep that night.

Chapter 27

"Hey, when's your next doctor's appointment?" Jake asked.

"Umm, it's next Thursday afternoon actually, why what's up?" I asked.

"Did you want me to go with you?" he asked.

"Really? Wow, I'm surprised you'd want to," I said.

"Well, I want to be there for you Zen. I told you a couple of months ago if you needed anything I'd be here for you," he responded.

Jake had actually been amazing through this entire thing. When I decided to keep the baby and told Isaiah, he flipped out. Come to find out, he was separated, but he and his wife were now talking about reconciling, which he never told me about. The lady friend I saw him out and about with—I found out *that* was his wife. She had come to visit without the kids to get a feel for the city, because she was thinking about relocating.

When I told Jake I was pregnant, he said it hurt him but he'd be by my side if I needed and wanted him. That he has been, helping me around the house, helping shop for the baby; he's been great! I never would've thought...

Now, five months pregnant, Isaiah was not really in the picture. As far as I was concerned, that was fine with me. This baby was already loved. I had no business messing with him anyway. After each doctor's appointment I would sometimes send him a text letting him know the progress.

"I'll let you know about next week. My mom did say she'd meet me there," I told him. "Jake, thank you. I know you don't have to do anything for me. I don't take anything you're doing for granted."

Jake smiled and said, "Zen, you're welcome. I know this is not the ideal situation, but I said I loved you and I want to show you just how much."

He walked into the kitchen to put some things away and left me on the couch. At that moment, I saw just how blessed I was to have people in my life that loved me this much. My parents, Amy, Jake…heck, even Sarah.

After finding out I was indeed pregnant, it was pretty scary for me. I'm pregnant with a child and the father now acts as if he doesn't know me; and he is reconciling with his wife. I fell for the oldest trick in the book and now I had to deal with the consequences.

To my knowledge, Isaiah's wife did not know about the baby yet. The last I spoke with him, he was trying to get me to end the pregnancy; which didn't end well for him.

But, what I decided to do was make the best of the situation and make lemonade with the lemons that were thrown at me. I decided to be happy and that was the best decision I could've made.

The things I was worried about in the beginning, no longer worried me. My biggest worry was my job; after speaking with my boss, he has been one of the most supportive people in my circle as well.

My other worry was how people would look at me for being a single parent with a father who was not really in the picture. But, there were great men in my circle that my child could look up to, to know exactly what a man looks like.

In the beginning of the pregnancy, I was depressed a little. I stopped going out and I stopped working out completely. I didn't care about my appearance any longer. It was nothing for me to stay in the house all weekend and not come back out until Monday morning to head into work. Amy saw the pattern and sat me down and helped me get out of the slump she saw I was falling in. I loved her even more for that.

After our talk, I was enjoying the space I was in at the moment as well. I was soaking up the attention I was getting from everyone. I was sure the attention would shift when the baby was born.

Jake came back into the living room with my favorite cake from the bakery down the street, but instead of just a slice, he bought the entire Red Velvet Cheesecake. That was another thing I was taking full advantage of, eating whatever I wanted to eat with no regrets.

"Oh, my GOD, Jake, you didn't have to get an entire cheesecake, but I sure am glad you did!" I said while stuffing my face.

Jake was laughing at the way I was eating.

Straight No Chaser: The Beginning

"Yeah, I see. Is it that good? I've never had their cheesecake before," he said.

"Oh, my goodness, take a piece. Don't let me eat this by myself. I can't believe I didn't turn you on to this when we were together," I said.

"You know I don't eat a lot of sweets," he said.

"Oh, yeah, I'm sorry about that. But you have to try this one. It's amazing!" I said.

"I don't want a whole piece, I may not like it," he said.

"Man! Take a bite of mine, lil baby," I said jokingly.

I fed Jake a piece of the cheesecake and his eyes closed.

"Seeeee, I told you! Good right!?" I exclaimed.

"I don't think I've ever had this kind of reaction to a piece of food before. I'm turning into you!" he said laughing.

"Stick with me kid, I can show you a few things," I said smiling.

We both laughed and Jake began to gaze at me for a second.

"What? What is it? Do I have food on my face?" I asked.

"No. I'm just looking, nothing major," he said.

"Oh, okay," I said, as I went back eating the cheesecake.

Straight No Chaser: The Beginning

I don't know what it was about him being here, but I think I was falling for him again. Maybe it was the influx of hormones that I acquired with this pregnancy, but I'm not sure exactly how I felt about this. But, he was proving himself to be worthy of another shot. I don't think he was seeing anyone else, especially spending so much time here. But, that really didn't mean much of anything to me. People do make time for what they want to make time for. Who knows what he does after leaving my house.

"Did you have someone else coming over later?" he asked.

"I think Amy said she would try and drop by later, but she never said what time. Why, what's up?" I asked.

"Well, I wanted to know if you would like to get out of the house to get something to eat, maybe?" he asked.

Jake had asked me a few times before to go out to eat, but I really didn't feel like going anywhere. I think he thought I was trying to avoid being out with him.

"Sure. What did you have in mind?" I asked.

"Really? I didn't have anything in mind. I was honestly expecting you to turn me down again," he said laughing.

"Well, you better figure it out then," I said laughing.

"Don't worry, I will. I have some errands I need to run before doing anything, but would 7 PM be ok?" he asked.

"Yeah, that'll be fine with me," I said.

Straight No Chaser: The Beginning

"Okay, well, I'll finish putting that toy together and I'll be back to pick you up," he said.

"Sounds like a plan," I said.

I knew it was early, but I wanted the baby's toy put together as soon as possible. It was so cute in the store and I didn't want to wait any longer.

While he was doing that, I decided to vacuum the house and clean my bathroom. Hopefully, Jake wouldn't give me too much grief. Nobody likes for me to do anything anymore. If they could walk for me, they probably would!

When I walked into my room I realized I hadn't checked my phone all day. When I looked at it, I saw I had a lot of missed calls for a Saturday. I listened to my voicemail. The first message was from Isaiah.

When I heard his voice, my heart almost stopped. The message itself really almost made my heart stop. He said he wanted us to meet up and talk. Really? Now, you want to talk! This was going to be interesting. Was I going to meet him? I was curious to see what he wanted. I listened to the rest of my messages and got to work cleaning.

After I got into my groove of cleaning, it dawned on me how much I had neglected my cleaning duties again. I should've been ashamed of myself. I'm just glad my mother wasn't here to see how dirty everything was; because I know she would've had more than enough to say about it.

Straight No Chaser: The Beginning

After I turned the vacuum off, I heard the doorbell ringing. I wonder how long it had been ringing. I looked through the peephole to see Amy standing on the other side of the door. I opened the door and saw she had bags in her hands.

"I know you said not to buy anything else, but, I couldn't help it," she said.

I rolled my eyes at her and burst out laughing.

"Well, let's see what you got this time," I said.

"Just a little something," she said.

"Ok, just a little something and you come in with five bags FULL of stuff!" I said shaking my head. Oh, my God, this is so cute!"

"Told ya!" she said. Is that Jake's car in the drive way?" she asked.

"Yeah, he's in the baby's room putting together a toy I found this week." I said.

When I glanced up at her, she was giving me this look.

"What?" I said.

"Nothing. Hey, Jake!" she yelled.

"Hey, what's going on Amy?" he yelled from the next room.

Amy looked back at me smiling.

"I don't know what you're smiling at but…" I said.

Jake walked back in the room.

"Okay, lil lady, the toy is now together and I will see you at 7," he said walking towards the door.

"Wait, you guys are going out tonight?" Amy asked.

"Yeah, she finally said yes," Jake said.

"Ha, ha. Y'all are not funny." I said. See you later, man!"

Jake closed the door behind him.

"I don't care what you were about to say before he walked back in the room, but I knew you two were on the road to getting back together," Amy said.

"We are not," I said abruptly. He's not even trying to go there. This is dinner between friends."

"Okay, friends," Amy said.

We walked into the baby's room to see the end result and I cried, just like I did when I was in the store. Amy looked at me and laughed.

We walked back into the living room and Amy walked into the kitchen likes she always does when she comes over.

"Oh yeah!" I yelled. "There's cheesecake on the coffee table."

Amy rushed back into the room with a bottle of wine in her hand.

"WHERE!? Oh, my goodness…gimme, gimme!" she said. When'd you get this?" she asked cutting her slice.

"Jake just bought it today," I told her.

"Girl, I don't care what you say. Why don't you two just get back together already? I think he's learned his lesson. I mean, he spends most days here with you helping you out. Although I was pissed with him before, he really has stepped up for you," Amy said.

She put the first bite of the cheesecake in her mouth and closed her eyes and did a little happy dance. I laughed at her because I have those reactions all the time when I eat anything.

"How are your parents, Zen?" Amy asked.

"They're good. I haven't seen or heard from them this week, which is shocking. They probably picked up and went out of town or something. The life of retirees," I said.

"Must be nice. I can't wait to retire," she said. "I am tired of working!"

"Same here and when the baby gets here I know I'll be over it, for sure. Well, how's your man doing? I assume still treating you well," I said smiling.

"That indeed he is. You know we went out of town last weekend to this vineyard in the mountains. We had the best time and we actually already made plans to go back," she said.

"That sounds so peaceful. I need a little get-away. The beach. The mountains. Heck, I'd even settle to stay in town at one of the hotels downtown," I said. Complete with a masseuse."

"Well, maybe Jake can make that happen for you. You know, I'm still surprised at him taking care of you while carrying some other man's baby," she said.

"I know, right. I told him that earlier, actually. I wanted to make sure he knew I wasn't taking anything he was doing for granted."

"Good for you. And you still hadn't heard from Isaiah?" she asked.

"OH girl, I knew it was something I forgot to tell YOU!!! Forgive my pregnancy brain. He called and left a message asking if we could meet and talk."

"About what? What a butthole he is," she said, laughing.

"Who knows? I'll take my time returning the phone call, because I'm in no hurry to talk to him. As far as I know he and his wife are back together," I said.

"Oh yeah, I forgot you told me that," she said. Well, sweetie, I don't want you getting yourself worked up about him. I know this is hard to do without him, but that's why you have us. People that are happy to help you with no question."

"And I appreciate it, you just don't know! I'd be a complete nut case without y'all," I said.

"You're already a nut case!" Amy said laughing. So, what are you wearing on your date tonight?"

I cut my eye at her and said, "It's not a date! And I don't know yet. I hadn't been anywhere in a while so I don't know what is going to fit me."

"Oh, well let's go find out what we can piece together then!" Amy said. Are you still wearing heels or did you retire those until after the baby is born?"

I laughed and said, "Yeah, I'm still tipping around in them as much as I can until my feet begin to swell."

Amy was riffling through my closet putting cute pieces together for me to try on.

"Let's keep in mind I like to eat so whatever I wear has to also be comfortable, not to mention cute," I said.

After the third outfit, I was getting frustrated. Everything was cute, just not comfortable enough and I refused to go buy something.

"Okay, lady bug, try this and let us hope for the best," Amy said.

"Whoa, we may have a winner, girl! Check me out!" I said modeling in my bedroom. It's super comfortable and super cute. As long as I've had these pieces, I wouldn't have thought to put them together."

"Ha! I'm the woman!" Amy exclaimed.

"Yes, Lucy Pearl, you are indeed the woman," I said. Now, I just hope he picks a great restaurant. I'll have a few in mind, just in case."

I was actually getting excited about our outing.

"Alright mama, I'm going to head out so you can get ready. Thanks for the cheesecake and wine. Call me later," Amy said.

I walked her to the door and watched her leave. I straightened the living room and began to get ready.

Chapter 28

Jake and I walked into the Jamaican restaurant and, surprisingly, for a Saturday night, it wasn't busy. A plus for me, because this mama was starving—but what was new?

The hostess escorted us to our table and took our drink orders. As we settled into our seats, there was awkward silence between us, then we burst out laughing.

"Listen, Jake, thank you for getting me out of the house, I appreciate it more than you know."

"No problem. I'm glad you accepted my invitation...this time," he said.

"Yeah. I think I said 'no' all of those times because I didn't want to chance confusing things," I admitted.

"I understand. But, I've been telling you, even before the baby that I wanted you and I back together. No, this is not my ideal situation, and people think I'm crazy. But, I know this is where I belong."

He was about to make me cry. I felt my eyes fill with water and a tear dropped before I could catch it.

"Dang it, I'm sorry. That was really sweet. I'm sure everyone thinks you're crazy; heck I think you're crazy some days to be honest. But, I'm also grateful and owe you," I said.

"No worries. You're my priority and I want and choose to be here," he said.

Straight No Chaser: The Beginning

The waitress came with our drinks and took our order.

"Excuse me, I have to use the restroom," I said.

On my way to the bathroom, I saw Isaiah and his wife sitting at the table I had to pass to get to the restroom. He was facing me. Our eyes met.

"Hi, Isaiah." I said. How are you?"

He looked at me nervously. He glanced at my belly, then quickly back to me. This was our first time seeing each other since I threw him out of my house.

"Heeey Zen, Xenia. I'm well, how are you?" he asked nervously.

"I'm well." I said smiling.

"Xenia, this is my wife, Keely," he said.

"Hi, Keely, nice to officially meet you," I said.

She gave me a half smile and said, "Nice to meet you."

"Well, you guys have a good night," I said.

I walked into the bathroom and had to throw water on my face to get myself together. I decided to go a different path back to my table.

I finally made it back to my seat. Jake saw that something was wrong.

"What happened?" he asked.

Straight No Chaser: The Beginning

"Isaiah's here," I said with a blank look.

Because Isaiah hadn't been around, he wasn't one of Jake's favorite people at the moment. I appreciated that, it showed me he truly had my back and he cared.

"Where?" he asked.

"Nope, I'm not telling you. It's okay, he's with his wife, so no need to make a scene IF that's what you were thinking. I'm cool, so you be cool," I demanded.

Things were a little tense after Jake found out he was there.

"Of all the restaurants in town, I just had to choose this one," Jake said laughing and shaking his head.

"Yeah, well, it's okay, you're cool, I'm cool. Right?" I asked again.

"Mmmmhmm, I'm cooler than a fan," he said.

We both started to laugh. I looked up and saw the couple of the hour walking towards us to leave.

"See ya, Zen!" Isaiah said waiving.

This time, I didn't say anything I gave him a half smile and continued to eat my Curry Goat.

"See, told ya I was cool," Jake said.

I gave him a hi-five and we finished dinner. After dinner, he surprised me and we went for a walk in the downtown area and stopped by a spot playing live music. I'm glad I wore some comfortable shoes. I loved listening to live music, but it was weird not having a drink while I sat and listened.

The band was amazing that night. It was a local jazz fusion group that I'd heard before, but I hadn't heard them in about a year. They sounded great then, but they sounded even more amazing tonight.

I don't know what it was about tonight, but if I believed in things being perfect, tonight would be it. I no longer felt bad about the situation I had gotten myself into. I no longer lost sleep over the fact that I was going to be a single mother. I rested in knowing, the people that needed to be in my life, were in my life at this very moment. I was grateful and felt blessed because there were people in my same predicament that didn't have that support.

After the band finished playing for the night, I glanced down at my watch to see the time. I hadn't glanced at the time all night and I couldn't believe what time it was!

"Dang, you've kept me out way after my bed time, Sir," I said to Jake.

"Really? I lost track of time, what time is it?" he asked.

"It's after 2 AM!" I said, laughing.

"Wow, well, let's get you home. I wanted to introduce you to a friend of mine," he said looking around.

I didn't know what to expect as he was looking around the venue.

"Oh, there he is," he said waving.

This handsome young man walked over to our table. It was one of the guys from the band.

"Zen, this is my boy, Rodney," he said.

I extended my hand and said, "Hi, Rodney, nice to meet you. You guys sounded amazing tonight. I'm a big fan."

"Wow, thanks for that," he said.

"Hey man, thanks for coming out to support," Rodney said to Jake.

"Man, no problem. Thanks for letting me know, it set our night off," Jake said. "But, hey I know you gotta pack up your stuff, I just wanted to let you know I did come out. Give me a call next week, maybe we can get together for drinks."

"Sounds good man. Zen, it was nice meeting you." Rodney said, walking back to the stage.

"Wow, you know people in high places I see. Jake, thanks for tonight. I really needed this."

"I know! Why do you think I've been trying to get you out of the house?" he said smirking.

"Yeah, yeah, yeah. Well, you were right—this time," I said.

As we walked back to the car, we talked more about life, our dreams and what we wanted to do with our futures. By the time we got back to the car, my feet were screaming!

"Oh, my gosh, my feet are killing me!" I said.

"Yeah, well I can't carry you," he said joking.

"You wouldn't carry me, even if I begged?" I asked.

"Nope." he said.

"Hmph. I hear you," I said taking off my shoes.

"I'm kidding. I would carry you, IF you asked," he asked.

"I'll keep that one in mind." I said looking at him smiling.

Before dropping me off at home, we stopped to get Krispy Kreme donuts.

"YES!!! The light is on! Thank you donut gods!" I exclaimed.

Jake almost killed us pulling into the parking lot. It seemed like he crossed 3 lanes of traffic to get there!

"SLOW DOWN!! Man, you have a pregnant lady in the car," I said laughing.

"Yeah, but like you said the light was on, I had to get here," he said.

We ordered our donuts and he drove me home. After pulling into the drive way, he opened my door and walked me into the house. Before leaving, he walked through the house to make sure everything was how I left it.

I walked him back to the door.

"Thanks, Jake, for a great evening. Thank you for taking my mind off everything for a few hours," I said.

I hugged him. Hard.

"You're welcome Zen. You don't have to keep thanking me," he said hugging me back. It was really my pleasure.

"I know. You know my hormones are jacked up," I said, laughing.

"Oh yeah, I forgot about that," he said. Well, everything looks good in here, so, I'll give you a call tomorrow?"

"Yeah, give me a call tomorrow," I said.

He kissed me on the cheek and I closed the door behind him. After closing the door, I leaned against it, taking in what transpired throughout the night, which made me smile.

I took my phone out of my purse and sent Amy a quick text.

Everything went great. I had a great time! Even saw Isaiah at the Jamaican restaurant and it didn't really phase me. I'll tell you about that one later.

Chapter 29

About a month later, Isaiah and I finally synced schedules so we could "talk." This should be an interesting meeting. Especially given the fact that he has not been around and has ignored me and my calls every chance he could.

I was at work one day and Sarah buzzed into my office.

"Zen, Isaiah is on the phone for you," she said.

There was a brief pause.

"Zen..." Sarah said.

"Yes, Sarah I'm here." I said taking a deep breath. Send him through."

I mustered up a smile before picking up the phone, so he wouldn't think I was in some kind of funk or had an attitude because he called.

"This is Xenia," I said.

"Well, hello there, Zen. It's Isaiah," he said.

"Oh, well, hello there. How can I help you today?" I asked.

"I was calling to see when we could get together and talk," he said.

"Sure, let me look over my calendar. I have some time this week actually around 2 PM if you're free to come to the office," I said.

"Oh, the office? I was thinking after work," he said.

I paused briefly and took deep breath.

"After work? How about Black Bean?" I asked.

"I was hoping to talk to you away from people," he said. Is your house off limits?"

"Actually, it is off limits," I said.

"Wow, okay. Can we meet at the park by the carousel?" he asked.

"Sure, sounds like a plan," I said. I'll be there around 5:30 PM."

"Okay, I'll see you then," he said.

I disconnected and didn't bother to say good-bye. I sat back in my chair and took a few deep breaths. Soon after, Sarah walked into my office.

"Zen, I just wanted to check on you," she said.

I didn't bother looking at her. I was looking out of my office window, choking back tears.

"I'm fine…" I said.

She didn't say anything else, I heard the door close and felt a tear escape from my eye.

"Damn hormones," I said out loud.

I wiped my tear and got back to work. Needless to say, I could hardly concentrate on my work. All I could think about was my meeting with Isaiah.

As I was packing up to leave for the day, I sent Amy a text letting her know what was going on.

> *Hey girl, meeting Isaiah after work at the park by the carousel. So, if I go missing, you know what to do.*

Part of me was kidding about the last part of the text, but just in case, I needed to cover my bases. I know he wasn't exactly happy about my keeping the baby and I'm sure that was what the conversation would partly be about.

"Sarah, I'm heading out to meet Isaiah. Just FYI, here's where I'm meeting him," I said. I handed her a piece of paper with the park's name written on it.

"Okay, thanks," she said. You think you'll be okay?" she asked.

"Yeah, I do, but just in case."

"Okay, I'll see you in the morning," she said slowly.

I waved and disappeared behind the elevator doors.

I couldn't help but to be nervous as I pulled into the parking lot. I felt my upper lip get wet with sweat. I looked in the rear view mirror to make sure everything looked okay.

When I was getting out of the car, my phone went off. I looked down to read the text, it was from Amy.

Straight No Chaser: The Beginning

Okay, gotcha, send me a pic of what you have on today. Good luck and remember don't look into his eyes. This is how we got into this in the 1ˢᵗ place ☺

I laughed at the last sentence and it was definitely true. I looked in the back seat for my flats so I could change my shoes. I snapped a picture for Amy and sent it to her.

As I was walking through the park, I took in the scenery. I smiled at the kids running after each other and playing with their friends.

I came to the carousel and there was no sign of Isaiah. I walked over to the pond to watch the ducks. I felt a tap on my shoulder and I froze for second.

"Hey, Zen, I didn't mean to startle you," he said. "Sorry I'm a few minutes late."

"Hi," I said.

We found a bench and sat in silence.

"You look amazing, Zen," he said.

"Gee, thanks. Swollen ankles or at least I think they are. I can't see my feet anymore," I snapped.

He didn't say anything.

"I know you're upset with me. I'm sorry for not being there for you and the baby—our baby…" he said.

I cut him off.

"MY baby. Remember, you want nothing to do with him or me," I said.

"It's a boy?" he asked.

I cut my eye at him and looked back at the carousel.

"Yes," I said.

"You can't look at me now?" he asked.

"Nope. I don't know who you are. I thought I knew, but that person obviously doesn't exist," I said. "You hurt me."

"I know. I apologize—for everything." he said.

"I know trying to reconcile with my wife didn't help," he said.

"I'm not upset about the reconciliation, I'm upset with your reaction to my being pregnant and your thinking there was only one solution," I said. "Did you even tell Keely about the baby?" I asked.

I finally turned and looked at him. It was his turn to look at the carousel and sit in silence.

"Yeah, that's what I thought," I said.

"She has suspicions that something more went on between us than just being colleagues," he said.

"How much longer are you going to keep this from her?" I asked.

"I know I've kept it from her long enough and I know I need to tell her, but this is a tough situation for me," he said.

"Imagine how I feel, actually carrying the baby and not having your support—at all!" I exclaimed. "Isaiah what is it that you want from me?"

There was silence for a few minutes after I asked this question.

"Let me be clear. I'm not asking for us to be together," I said.

"Okay. I guess, I'm asking to be in the baby's life?" he said slowly.

"You sure about that?" talking slowly, I asked..

"I'm sure, Zen. I just need time to get my words together so I can tell my wife and figure out how we're going to tell the kids," he said.

"Isaiah, I hate this is so messy. But, if you're serious about all of this, you need to tell her soon. The baby is almost finished cooking," I said. "We need to figure how we're going to co-parent this child."

He took a deep breath. I looked at him. He looked at me. We sat on the bench in silence for a few moments. I began to play with my hands. Whenever I played with my hands, that meant I was nervous or uneasy about something. Isaiah noticed.

"Zen, no need to be nervous," Isaiah said.

"No need? Are you kidding me? You're about to tell your wife I'm carrying your child and I shouldn't be nervous? Really!? How do you think she's going to react?" I asked.

"Not good. Honestly, we're in a good place, she and the kids are preparing to move here. She's going to flip," he said.

"Just so she doesn't try coming after me, then we're good," I said.

"No, she wouldn't do that," Isaiah assured me.

We watched the kids play in the park and sat in silence. I felt Isaiah looking at me.

"What is it?" I asked not looking at him.

"Nothing. Well, not really nothing, but I don't want you to think I'm a horrible person. I got scared that night and panicked," he said.

I didn't say anything because I felt a lump forming in my throat and my eyes began to water. I tried hard to hold back tears but it didn't work for long.

"I'm sorry, Zen," he said.

I nodded my head and turned my head so he couldn't see me wipe a tear away.

"Listen, I gotta go. Can we finish this up later?" I asked getting up.

"Now? I was hoping we could get a bite and start putting together a plan," he said.

I don't know what happened, but I flipped! Now he wants to be swoop in and be super dad!?

"You are a piece of work! One day you're telling me to get rid of it, now you want to draw up plans?!" I yelled.

"Zen, lower your voice, people are looking," he said.

"Let them!" I exclaimed. "You can't come six months later and think everything is going to be easy now."

I couldn't take it anymore, so I turned around and rushed towards my car. Isaiah followed, calling my name, but trying not to yell too loud.

When I got to my car, I had to fumble in my purse for my keys.

"Zen, wait. You can't run away from this. What's important is I'm here now," he said.

"Oh, I know I can't run away from this! But, you on the other hand…" I said before he cut me off.

"I'm here now and I'm sorry," he said.

I stood there in utter shock at *how quickly* he thought I should forgive him for leaving and not checking on me the past six months. I couldn't hold it together any longer, I began to cry—uncontrollably. He held his arms open to hug me. I didn't want him touching me, but I needed a hug and for someone to hold me as reassurance that things would be okay.

"You're either all in or you're not," I told him through my sobbing. You need to be about action, I'm not moved by your words any more Isaiah. I know this isn't the situation we wanted to be in, but we're in it."

"I know, Zen. I know," he said calmly.

His hug calmed me down. We stood there in silence as tears rolled down my face. My hormones were haywire! I couldn't help but feel a little embarrassed by my sobbing. As I stopped sobbing, he looked at me and smiled.

"Zen, I'm here. I know I left months ago, but I'm here. I want to be in this child's, our child's life. I want him to know his father," he said.

I looked at him wiping my tears. This time, I didn't match his smile. I was serious about being about action and not just saying what he *wanted* to do.

"I want that as well. I don't want you thinking I'd try to keep you from your child, because I wouldn't do that. I just need you to be there for him, nothing else," I said.

I looked at him and he looked at me. Silence overtook us. Then, he leaned in to kiss me. I turned my head.

"Isaiah," I said shaking my head. That…isn't going to happen again. I fell for it once, not again."

"You're right. I apologize," he said.

"Listen, I gotta go," I said looking at him.

"Okay. Maybe we can sit down again over dinner and draw up a plan before the baby gets here," he said.

"Yeah," I said getting into my car.

I drove away and watched him disappear in my rear view mirror.

Chapter 30

The baby had grown faster than I thought and I couldn't believe my belly could actually stretch that far! Now, eight months pregnant, I couldn't believe the end was drawing near. All I could think about, at this point, was getting my body back. I missed being able to see my feet, bend over, put my own shoes on; you know, the things you take for granted while not being pregnant.

Oh, and how could I forget the awesome, attractive waddle that I had become accustomed to for the past two months?

I hurt in places I never knew could hurt or even existed. I couldn't find comfortable positions so I could sleep at night. But, one of the most amazing things was watching the baby move inside my belly. I couldn't believe it, the first time it happened. I was sitting in church one Sunday and Amy pointed it out to me; needless to say, after that, we were no longer paying any attention to service. We were in awe.

Isaiah was pretty much still absent, even after we met in the park. We never met for dinner to draw up a co-parenting plan, like he said he wanted. He claimed to be swamped with work. He only called once to really talk and check in on the baby's progress. By now, I'm sure his wife and kids had moved to the city.

I'm glad I didn't get my hopes up. I couldn't afford to stress out about him anymore because I had the baby's health to consider. More importantly, I didn't want to go into early labor worrying over his lack of support. Although, it would have been nice to have his support, I had all I needed from my circle.

"Zen, girl, it's your mama. How are you doing today? Feeling okay?" she asked.

"Hey mama, I'm doing okay. How are you?" I asked.

"Oh, chile, I'm good. I'm a little tired today and not sure why," she replied.

"Well, are you eating good?" I asked.

"Girl, yeah, I am," she said. She sounded annoyed with the question.

"Well, I know how you are sometimes. You don't like to eat balanced meals and regardless of what you say, it's good for your health," I said.

"You always trying to run me. I'm YOUR mama, not the other way around," she said.

I laughed and said, "Okay, mama. How's daddy?" I asked.

"He's good. He's outside cutting grass right now. How's that grandbaby? Still cooking?" she asked.

"Yes, ma'am…still cooking, thank God. He's been giving me heartburn the past week."

"Well, they say if you have heartburn, the baby will have a head full of hair," she said.

"Really? Wow, well we shall see in a few weeks," I said.

"I know and I can't wait. Listen, baby, I know you may not want to talk about it…" she said.

Oh, Lord, I knew what she was going to talk about and she was right, I didn't want to talk about it.

"What is it, mama?" I said.

"Have you tried calling the baby's father?" she asked.

"No ma'am. Not since the last time we talked about him." I said. "Mama, he knows my number and where I live, thanks to you. If he's too busy for the baby now, he's definitely going to be too busy after he's here. The ball is in his court now. I've already told him I wouldn't keep him from his child. He needs to make the effort."

There was silence and I knew what it meant.

"Okay, baby, I just want the baby to know his father, that's all," she said.

"I do too, but, I can't make him. I know this is a sticky situation, but…" I said.

"I know baby," she said cutting me off.

"Mama, I love you and daddy so much. Thank you guys for being there for me these past few months. I know you both wanted more for me, but thank you for being there," I said.

"Awe girl, you're welcome. What did you think we were going to do, leave you in the cold?" she asked. Things happen and while this wasn't the ideal, it's too late to dwell on that, you just need to focus on that baby and doing right by him."

"Thanks, mama," I said. I'm going to call you guys later, I'm pulling into work."

"Alright baby," she said disconnecting the call.

My mama always knew what to say to make me feel a little better. I honestly hope I was as good of a mom as mine was.

I waddled into the building and when I got off the elevator, my staff was gathered around Sarah's desk. I stepped off the elevator and looked at them, wondering what was going on.

"Ummm, good morning, guys. Did I call a meeting and forget about it or something?" I asked slowly.

"Hey, Zen. No, you didn't!" Sarah said.

"Okay, well, why are you guys gathered around the desk like this," I asked. Need more work to do?"

I walked by Sarah's desk into my office. When I opened my door, I saw why they were gathered. They decorated my office for a mini baby shower.

When I turned around, they all shouted in unison, "SURPRISE!!!!!!"

I laughed and, of course, I cried.

"Y'all make me sick!! But, this is amazing!" I said.

They had blue balloons everywhere! I had never seen so many ducks and elephants in my life.

"Is that a Red Velvet Cheesecake," I asked.

They all knew how much I loved it.

"Yep," Sarah said. "Now sit down and open your gifts so we can eat."

I was glad the food was there because I was starving again! The staff chipped in and bought the baby a stroller and car seat set.

"You guys are amazing. I am truly amazed and shocked by all of this," I said.

After the excitement wore down and we were all full, everyone dispersed and went back to their offices to get their days started. After eating, I wasn't up to doing any work! I don't think anyone else was, either.

There was a knock on my office door.

"Come in," I yelled.

"Zen, I wanted to check on you," Sarah said.

"Yeah, come on in. Have a seat," I said.

She walked over with a huge smile on her face.

"I hope you enjoyed your surprise. I know how they're not really your favorite thing, but we thought it would be a good idea to show our appreciation," she said.

"No, they aren't my favorite. But, I'm glad you guys did this. I needed this today," I told her.

"I know you did. I noticed that your waddle is slowing down a tad bit. I wasn't sure if it's because of the situation itself or you're just tired," she said.

As hard as I tried to hide it, she was right. The situation had taken somewhat of a toll on me; I even noticed my waddle being slower. I just chalked it up to being further along.

"Get that cheesecake and bring it over here," I said.

We both had two more slices each. There were hardly ever days where I goofed off at work, but today just felt like a goof-off day. Sarah stayed in my office a majority of the day.

"So have you heard from Isaiah?" she asked slowly.

"Nope. Sure haven't and, at this point, I couldn't care less. It is what it is now. After we met at the park, I thought he was going to step up," I said.

"Same here. I'm sorry Zen, I thought he was one of the good guys," she said.

"You and me both, girl. He fooled us, but not again," I said.

"How about Jake? Have you guys talked about getting back together?" she asked.

"He's still amazing. We haven't officially talked about it, but if he were ask me, I'd seriously consider it now. He's shown me another side of him since I told him I was pregnant," I said.

Sarah's eyes lit up after I said that.

"Oh, Zen! I like Jake, I always have. If you two decide to work it out, I'm all for it," she said.

"Yeah, you and my mom," I said.

"Well, WE do know best," Sarah said laughing.

"Yeah, yeah, yeah. Y'all think you know what's best for me, huh? You thought Isaiah was good for me," I said laughing.

"Well, I missed that one," she said.

When I looked at my computer screen, I glanced down to see what time it was.

"Oh my gosh, it's time go home," I said.

"Dang, we really didn't do anything today but talk," Sarah said.

"Yeah, now I gotta go home and do the work I should've been doing today," I said laughing.

We walked out of the building together and parted ways. As I got closer to my car, I saw something on my windshield. I thought nothing of it. I thought it was an advertisement.

I placed everything in the backseat of my car. Before getting into the car I took what I thought was an advertisement off my windshield. It was a piece of folded notebook paper. I opened it to read the note. It was from Isaiah. In short, he wanted to meet after I left work.

I stood there holding this piece of paper in my hands. Sarah drove by and honked her horn good-bye. I waved and got into my car.

Was I going to meet him or just blow him off?

Why didn't he just come upstairs to talk to me? Better yet, he could've called! I put the key in the ignition and drove out of the parking lot. Half-way home, I decided to turn around and meet with him to see what his story was this time around.

I parked my car and got out and walked into the restaurant and saw him sitting at the table. I walked towards the table trying not to get upset.

"What…do you want," I asked.

"Hello to you too," he said.

I stood staring at him. I waited for him to answer my question.

"Zen, I'm…" he started…

I cut him off mid-sentence.

"Let me guess, you're sorry? Again?" I asked. Save your excuses because I don't want to hear them this time."

"Zen, I've been swamped with work and getting my family here has been more hassle than I thought," he said.

"Oh? What did your wife say when you told her about the addition to the family?" I asked.

Isaiah looked away in embarrassment. I shook my head at him.

"I can't believe you, you haven't told her," I said.

"Every time I sit her down with intentions of telling her, it doesn't come out," he said.

"That sounds like an excuse to me. Something I said I didn't want to hear," I said. I am pretty much due any day now, and your wife doesn't know a thing, and you've known the same amount of time I've known. Let me be clear, I'm no longer worried about you telling her—it's not my responsibility. But, if you're thinking about co-parenting lil man with me, I'm not sure how long you think keeping him a secret will last."

"Zen, I know this," he said.

"That's just it, you know everything! No one can tell you anything!" I exclaimed. "You have worked all of my nerves!!"

"Zen, Keeley is actually meeting us here so I can tell her." he said.

I stopped dead in my tracks. I think I held my breath for a little while.

"Who's meeting who? where?" I asked. "I'm confused."

"Keeley is meeting us here, I thought it would be best...." he said.

"...for *you*?" I said cutting him off mid-sentence. You aren't fooling me. You don't think she's going to fly off the handle in public with me here? You are absolutely bananas! Not only is she going to fly off the handle, but you're putting me in a potentially volatile situation? Un-freaking-believable!"

I couldn't take it anymore. How could someone so intelligent be this...dumb! I got up to leave the restaurant.

"Zen, you can't leave," he said.

I turned around with a stern look on my face.

"Watch..." I said.

I waddled out of the restaurant and as I opened the door, Keeley was coming through the door as well. She held the door for me, not realizing who I was.

"Oh, hi, Zen right?" she asked.

"Yeah, Keeley, right?" I replied.

"Yes. Looks like you're about to go any day now," she said.

"Yep, that's about right," I said. "It was nice seeing you."

I rushed out of the restaurant before Isaiah could catch up to me. I got into my car and left. As I was driving by the front, I saw Isaiah talking to Keeley.

Keeley didn't look too happy.

Things have officially gotten real.

Chapter 31

NOW in my last month, Isaiah and I still hadn't gotten a co-parenting plan together. He did finally tell his wife, Keeley, everything. As I predicted, she hit the roof! She even found and stalked my phone for about a week.

I never answered my phone when she called. She never left a message. What was I going to say? I know she was hurt. Had the shoe been on the other foot, I would've been hurt. I was still kicking myself for falling for this guy. Whether he was separated or not, he was still married.

I was putting things away in the baby's room when I heard a knock at the door. I walked into the living room and saw that Isaiah, true to form, stopped by unannounced. I opened the door without hesitation.

"Thanks for stopping by unannounced, again," I said.

"I stopped by to apologize for Keeley calling you like that. I begged her not to, but as you can see..." he said.

"Yeah, for a solid week. I understand to an extent—she's upset and I would be as well."

"So, can we talk?" he asked.

"We're talking. I'm not inviting you in, if that's what you're getting at," I said.

"Okay, well, can you come outside so we can talk?" he asked.

I picked up my cell phone and walked outside and leaned against my car.

"I can't keep doing this Zen," he said.

"Can't keep doing what?" I asked.

"This. The arguing back and forth. The passive aggressive behavior." he said.

This wasn't making sense at all to me.

"Is this what you really called me out here for!? The nerve of you. I can't keep doing it, either. The lies you tell, trying to build my hopes up making me think I'm actually going to have some help," I said.

Then the other shoe dropped.

"How do I even know this is my kid?" he said.

"The hell…this has to be Keeley putting this in your head. That's fine, no one wants this to be your baby, I get it. The baby is going to mess up your perfect family, right? Because a few months ago, you weren't questioning if this baby was yours," I said.

"I want a paternity test done," he said.

"You want it done or Keeley wants it done?" I asked abruptly.

He couldn't even look me in my eye when he asked.

I couldn't believe this guy. A paternity test? Now, my word isn't good enough for him? Hmph, okay!

"I have no reason to lie about this being your child. You, of all people, should know I don't hop beds and sleep with people casually. That's not me!" I said.

"I remember you telling me that, but how do I know for sure?" he asked.

I looked at him, smiled and shook my head. I honestly couldn't believe this guy is thinking that I'm trying to trap him. Yeah, this was exactly what I wanted for my life. To trap a married man to ignore me; one who obviously doesn't really have his stuff together. Yeah, that's what I wanted for my life—drama.

"It's cool, you want the test, you got it. And when it comes back saying this is your child, you won't have to worry about a thing," I said.

"What's that supposed to mean?" he asked.

I began to waddle towards the house.

"Bye, Isaiah, I'm done." I said.

He followed me to the door. When I got to the door I turned to face him.

"What?" I asked abruptly.

"What does that mean," he asked. Are you threatening me?"

"I don't make threats. Have a good night," I said.

Straight No Chaser: The Beginning

I closed the door behind me and leaned against the door. I listened for his car to start and pull out of my drive-way. After he pulled off, I called Jake.

"Hey you, how are you?" I asked.

"Hey Zen, what's wrong?" Jake replied.

"What? Nothing. Are you busy?" I asked.

"Not really I'm out with the boys," he said.

"Oh, shoot. Well, if you're up to it, stop by afterwards."

"Okay, I'll let you know," he said. We disconnected the call.

He knew something was wrong and I didn't want to come out and say Isaiah scared me a little.

My phone buzzed a few minutes later. I looked down and it was a message from Jake.

I know something's up. I'll be there in about an hour.

I smiled and put the phone back down. I walked into the kitchen to find something to snack on and I needed to find something to cook for later. The least I could do was have something to eat in the house when Jake got here. It would be my way of saying 'thank you' for cutting boys' night short.

"Hello?" I said answering the phone.

"Hey, Zen, girl, I wanted to check on you," Amy said.

"Hey girl, I'm cooking right now, waiting on Jake. And oh, check this out, Isaiah asked for a paternity test," I said.

"Wait. Hold it. Paternity test? Like, you sleep around? He knows better. So, what did you say?" she asked.

"Told him he could have it. He's not asking for it, Keeley's asking for it," I said. And I told him when it came back as his, I was done."

"Done? As in what?" she asked.

"As in, he doesn't have to have anything to do with the baby. But he will pay child support." I said. I'm not going to keep doing this with him."

"You aren't going to try and keep the baby from him are you?" she asked.

"God no! I told him I wouldn't do that, and I hadn't changed my mind. It's going to be up to the courts from this point forward," I said.

"Okay. Well, have you talked to a lawyer or have a lawyer in mind?" she asked.

"Not yet. It's on my growing list of things to do," I said. I would love to have this settled before the baby is born, but we both know I could go any day now."

"Yeah, well, I'll ask around for a good family lawyer for you and let you know what I find. But, moving on to a lighter topic, how are you feeling?" she asked.

Straight No Chaser: The Beginning

"Girl, I'm ready to have my body back. The baby's really active today. The doctor said he was in position and ready to go BUT I haven't dilated yet." I said.

"It's good he's in the correct position. I'm excited and ready to see my nephew. Oh yeah, I bought some stuff for him too!" she said.

"Girl, he is not in need of anything else. Between you and mama, he is set for the first year of his life," I said laughing.

"Yep, I know, but auntie loves her baby!!! Besides, I don't want you to have to worry about anything," she said. "I'm already planning to stay with you guys after you come home to help out around the house."

This is why I loved her. Selfless. I never had to ask her for anything, she just did it because that was the type of person she was. I couldn't wait to repay her.

"Amy, you know you don't have to do that, but I'm glad you are. I'm scared to death to be with the baby by myself," I said relieved.

"Girl, I'd be scared, too. Besides you're my family and you know I'll do just about anything for family. Especially when they deserve it," she said.

"I owe you a lot, girl. Hey, I'm almost finished cooking, why don't you come over," I asked.

"I thought you said that was for Jake?" she asked.

"He's cutting boys night short just to come over and I wanted there to be something here for him eat. You know I don't know how to cook for just two people, so there's plenty," I said.

"You asked him to cut boys night short?" she asked.

"Nope. I called and he said he was with them, I didn't ask him to come over. He sensed something was wrong when I called him and after we hung up, he sent me a text saying he'd be over later," I explained.

"That was nice of him. I am hungry, so what are you cooking?" she asked.

"Lasagna. And it's huge…so, please, come get some," I begged.

"Okay, I'll be over in fifteen minutes," she said hanging up.

It seemed as if Amy got to my house in five minutes instead of fifteen, I guess she was hungry or maybe I just lost track of time. She stopped by the bakery before coming to my house and bought fudge brownies and red velvet cake.

"Oh, yummers!! CAKE!" I exclaimed as she walked through the door.

"Yes, I had a taste for something fudgey and, of course, I got you the red velvet slices," she said.

"Girl, I didn't even know I wanted it, but thank ya, kindly," I said. The lasagna is still cooking, so, we have a few minutes."

"Cool!" she said walking into the kitchen.

"There's wine in the fridge! I yelled.

"How'd you know?" she asked.

"I know YOU!" I said laughing.

She came back with forks for our desserts. I loved eating dessert before my meals; I did it often and never felt bad about it.

"Did you tell Jake about Isaiah's request?" she asked sitting on the couch.

"Nah, not yet. I actually called him to ask him to spend the night, because Isaiah kind of scared me," I said.

"Scared you? Do we need to file a restraining order or something?" she asked concerned.

"No. At least, I hope not. Since the time I'd known him, he hadn't shown any signs of crazy. I just wanted to be sure and have him here in case he tried coming back later tonight," I said.

"Okay, well let me know if you change your mind," she said.

Straight No Chaser: The Beginning

We decided to watch our favorite movie while we waited for the lasagna to finish. We had watched *Love Jones*® so many times, we were actually acting out everyone's part!

There was a knock at the door and Amy went to see who it was. Jake had finally arrived. Amy opened the door for him.

"Hey, Jake!" Amy said.

"Hey, girl, what's up?" he asked. "Do I smell lasagna?" he asked.

"Yep. I figured since you cut your night short, I'd make something to say thanks for coming over," I said.

"Awe, man, thanks for that. We weren't eating anything, just at the bar drinking and eating peanuts and pretzels," he said.

"It's not done yet, it may have about thirty minutes," I said.

Jake walked into the kitchen for a beer and looked to see how long he had to wait to eat.

"It has about twenty minutes left and I can't wait," he said walking back into the living room.

"I brought brownies, too, Jake," Amy said.

"The food gods must be looking down on me *tonight*, because I'm having all of my food spots hit today," he said, smiling from ear to ear.

We all laughed.

Straight No Chaser: The Beginning

"Are y'all watching some chick flick?" he asked.

"Uh, *Love Jones®*? I wouldn't necessarily classify this as a chick flick," Amy said.

"Yes, yes it is. But, this is a cool movie," he said.

"Okay, y'all are talking way too much," I said.

The lasagna was finally done and we all fixed our plates and continued watching the movie.

After the movie went off, Amy left so I could update Jake about Isaiah. I was nervous, because I knew he'd fly off the handle.

"So, are you going to tell me what's wrong?" he asked.

I looked at him nervously.

"Is something wrong with the baby or you?" he asked, concerned.

"No, no it's not that. Isaiah came by earlier," I said.

Jake's whole demeanor changed, including his facial expression.

"What did he want?" he asked, sitting up on the couch.

I sat in silence for a few moments.

"He asked for a paternity test," I finally said.

Now was his turn to sit in silence as I sat on eggshells. I looked at him. He took our plates to the kitchen and stayed there for a while, not saying a word.

"Did he question if the baby were his a few months ago?" he asked.

"No…" I said.

"So how is he…oh. I get it. His wife is asking for it, right?" Jake asked.

"That's my exact thought. I guess if the shoe were on the other foot, I'd tell my husband to ask as well. But, before we started hanging out, I told him I didn't hop beds and he was cool," I said.

"This guy," he said shaking his head. "Well, what did you say?"

"I told him I'd have the test done, but after that I'm done. Amy's going to help me find a family lawyer. I won't keep him from seeing the baby, but I won't beg him to be around either," I said.

"Good for you. You have a good support system now, so even if he decides to not be around, I think you'll be okay." he said.

"Thanks, J."

"No problem, girl, you know I got your back," he said.

I smiled and nodded in agreement. We decided to watch another movie until we dozed off.

Chapter 32

I had been feeling bad all day at work and all I wanted was my bed and to sleep. I was nauseated and my entire body ached. After complaining for about two hours, Sarah suggested I call my doctor to be on the safe side.

My doctor called me into her office and examined me and to my surprise I had dilated three centimeters!

"Congrats, lady bug, you're in labor," she said.

I immediately got nervous. I was ready, but I wasn't ready, and it was too late. I mean,,I had another week for him cook.

"I'm not due for another week, isn't it too soon?" I asked.

My doctor laughed and said, "Relax, he is going to be fine coming a week early. I know you're nervous, but everything is going to fine. Trust me."

I looked at her with a stunned look on my face.

"But, how can I be dilated and my water hasn't broken yet? That doesn't sound normal," I said.

"It doesn't, but it is; I assure you," she said. But, I'm going to send you home and when your contractions get closer then we'll admit you and it'll be show time."

She smiled at me like everything was cool. Nothing about this was cool or going to be cool. If I felt like this now at three centimeters, I could imagine how I was going to feel at ten!

I left the doctor's office and went back to work to start executing my maternity leave plan.

"Oh, my gosh, I'm getting excited Zen!" Sarah said.

"Calm down, you have to help me get everything together in case I'm not here, starting tomorrow. Everyone knows their job when I go out on leave; we're just now putting everyone on notice. Make sure you contact everyone with a phone call first, then follow up with an email and copy me on it," I told her.

"I'm on it," she said walking back to her desk.

I called my boss to let him know what was going on and he was excited as well.

"Xenia, why are you back at work if you're almost ready?" he asked.

"I have to make sure everything is in order before I leave just in case," I told him.

"I'm sure your team is more than prepared and can handle your not being here. Hurry up and get out of here and rest, because after the baby is here, rest is something you're going to beg for from this point forward," he said, laughing.

"Yes sir. And sir, thank you for your support," I said. "I'm sure I'll be at work tomorrow, but I will definitely keep you posted."

After hanging up, I looked out of the window, taking deep breaths as I contracted.

"Okay, lil guy, I hope you're ready because it's rock and roll time and mommy can't wait to hold you," I said, talking to my belly.

I almost forgot to call my mama to put her on notice as well. After I thought about it, I decided against it and would call on the way to the hospital. My mom could be a bit much in situations where you needed her to be calm.

I picked up my phone and sent Isaiah a text letting him know I had started to dilate.

Hey...just fyi...I've dilated 3 cm. I'll keep you posted.

I wasn't expecting him to respond as quickly as he did, but, surprisingly, he did.

Ok, are you feeling ok? Do you need anything? Are you at work or home? Thanks for letting me know.

He called before I had the opportunity to reply to his text.

"I couldn't wait on the text," he said when I answered the phone.

"Yeah, I see. But, I'm ok and, yes, I'm at work, getting things in order in case I'm not here tomorrow," I said.

"Okay, cool. Cool..." he said.

There was a brief pause.

"Well, I'll let you know when the baby's born and the test has been completed. I have to go, Sarah just came in."

I was trying to rush him off the phone because it was getting awkward! I lied to get him off the phone.

"Okay, I'll look forward to your call," he said.

I hung up before he could say good-bye. Even though I was in pain all day, my team finally kicked me out of the office at 4 PM.

We hugged each other and I told Sarah to have her phone handy just in case. I left and picked up something to eat before heading home.

I called Amy on the way home and let her in on the excitement. She was more than upset with me that I waited all day to call her, but I bribed her with food so she wouldn't be too upset.

When I pulled into the driveway, she and Jake were waiting on me. I got out of the car laughing at them both.

"What are you laughing at?" she asked.

"You guys. I can't believe you both beat me here," I said.

"Well, we're excited!" Jake said taking the bags from my hands.

I stopped walking for a moment. I was having another contraction. It seemed as if Jake and Amy held their breath the entire time.

"Are you okay?" she asked with her eyes wide open.

"Yes…" I said, breathing slowly.

We walked into the house and I went to change clothes. When I walked back into the living room, I had my hospital bag with me and placed it on the table next to the door.

"You really think you're going tonight?" Amy asked.

"I'm not sure, but I brought it up just in case. When I am ready to go, I don't want to not be able to find it or you guys to not be able to find it," I said.

"Sounds like you're prepared," Jake said.

"Yeah, to get out of the house and to the hospital, but not this parenting thing," I said.

I was having another contraction that I was trying to breathe through. I closed my eyes and pressed my head back on the couch.

"Okay, I think it passed. These contractions are something else," I said.

I looked at both Jake and Amy and they looked as if they were about to pass out!

"Are y'all okay? I mean…" I said.

"No, no, no…we're fine," Amy said—lying.

"Lies!" I said and laughed. "All you guys have to do is keep me calm and focused on breathing."

"Okay, well, are you hungry? If so, I'll go ahead and fix you something," Jake said.

I nodded as he walked to the kitchen to fix our plates. Before coming home I stopped at an Italian spot for Cajun Chicken Alfredo and I couldn't wait to eat it.

"Did you call your mama, yet? You know she's going to flip when you do finally call!" Amy said.

"No, I haven't. You know mama can be a bit extra in situations like this. I'll have one of you call when I get to the hospital," I said.

Jake and Amy looked at each other and then again at me and rolled their eyes in sync.

"Did you just roll your eyes at me?" I asked laughing.

"Why are you giving *US* this job? I don't want your mom yelling at me!" Jake said.

"You can handle it…" I said.

I was having another contraction. I was trying to ignore them and eat at the same time, but it wasn't working. After we finished eating, we walked the neighborhood. As we were walking, I'd have contractions and would bend over to breathe through them.

It was hilarious because cars were slowing down to see if I was okay. Amy waved to them, letting them know I was alright. We kept walking and laughing.

Straight No Chaser: The Beginning

We finally made it back to the house and Jake and Amy made the executive decision to take me to the hospital because the contractions were getting closer.

I had butterflies in my stomach and little man was kicking me like crazy. I guess he was ready to make his appearance. When we arrived at the hospital, my doctor was already there, delivering babies. I was so glad to see her when she walked into the room to check on me.

"Okay, lady bug, how are you feeling?" she asked.

"I'll be better when the baby is out of me," I said.

She laughed and said, "I know how you feel. Let's see what's going on here."

She checked to see how far I had dilated from earlier in the day. She also did an ultrasound.

"Is everything okay" I asked.

The silence was making me a little uneasy. I'm glad Amy was with me. We left Jake in the waiting room and he was glad about that.

"Yes, ma'am, you are now seven centimeters and I'm going to have you admitted," Dr. Sharon said smiling. We're going to have a baby tonight!"

She walked out of the room and I was getting more and more anxious. Amy and I looked at each other with smiles on our faces.

I got up to change into my gown and asked Amy to go ahead and have Jake to call my parents. When she left the room, I sent Isaiah a text letting him know I was in labor and being admitted. I also sent Sarah a text to let her know as well.

Amy came back into the room smiling and didn't say anything.

"What is it?" I asked.

"Girl, I told Jake you were being admitted and he shed a little tear. I know this may not be the right time to talk about this, but I hope you guys talk about getting back together," she said.

"It's not the right time, but I'll keep that in mind," I said shaking my head.

We both laughed until another contraction hit me. Amy was doing great helping me focus on my breathing. An hour passed and my doctor came back in to check my cervix.

"Alright, young lady! We are now at about seven and half centimeters." she said.

"Is that ALL!?" I exclaimed. "It feels like my uterus is about to tear out of my body and I've only dilated half a centimeter."

"It's okay, just breathe. These things take time, everything will be okay," she said rubbing my leg.

She strolled out of the room like everything was fine and cool. But she wasn't the one getting ready to push something the size of a watermelon out of something the size of a kiwi!

"Oh my gosh, this epidural doesn't seem like it's working," I said to Amy.

I looked at Amy and she looked scared to death!

"Girl, get it together!" I demanded.

"I'm sorry, this is too much! We are not having kids any time soon," she said.

I laughed through my next contraction at her comment. Yes, this was great birth control.

"Yes ma'am, take your birth control on time every day," I said laughing. This is not fun!!"

By this time, my mom burst into the room. Part of her was mad I didn't call when I went to the doctor's that morning and the other part was too happy to care.

"Oh, my baby is having a baby!" she exhaled.

"Hey, mama…" I said breathing through another contraction.

She went to wash her hands before touching me or anything else in the room.

"Hey, Amy, how has she been doing?" she asked.

"She's been doing fine. I've been trying to help her focus on her breathing," she said.

Straight No Chaser: The Beginning

"I had a contraction a few minutes ago and she said she wasn't having kids mama," I said.

My mom laughed at her.

"Well, baby, children will change your life in a good way. They will definitely put things into perspective," she said. The things you used to care about won't matter."

"You're right mama," I said.

As I was lying there contracting, I was thinking back to the stupid stuff I thought was important before, but now, seemed so minute—especially, the arguments and disagreements with Isaiah.

I kept looking at my phone waiting for Isaiah to respond to my text, but he never did. Well, he knew, all I could do now was push when it was ready.

Another hour passed and I hadn't seen my doctor, but there were plenty of nurses coming in and out of the room with ice chips.

My contractions were getting closer and more intense. I didn't think they could get any more intense than they had already been. By this time the doctor came back into the room.

"I'm so glad to see you. I know I have got to be ready to push now," I said to Dr. Sharon.

She got everything ready to check my cervix again. At that moment I thought to myself, I was never sleeping with anyone else again. Amy was right, this was too much!

Straight No Chaser: The Beginning

"Alright, lady bug! We are ready to rock and roll! When I get back in, we're going to start pushing this baby out, okay?" Dr. Sharon said.

"Thank you Jesus!!! Okay…" I said.

She disappeared behind the door. Not that they weren't before, but mama and Amy *really* began to pray over me for a safe delivery.

When Dr. Sharon came back in, she was dressed in her delivery gown and cap. The nurses helped to get me into position and Amy and mama were on both of my sides holding my hands.

"Whatever I say or do, please don't hold it against me okay?"

They both smiled and nodded.

"Okay, sweetie, on my count we're going to push," Dr. Sharon said.

I was scared to death, but I was ready! I pushed when I needed to. After pushing for almost an hour, I was exhausted. This is the stuff people never tell you about. How many people will be in your personal space, how long you may have to push, how long it takes to dilate!!! Oh, my gosh!!!

I was so exhausted, all I wanted to do was go to sleep. Amy and my mom were so supportive.

"Okay, the next contraction I need you to give me a big push, sweetheart!" Dr. Sharon said.

Straight No Chaser: The Beginning

"Oh, God, can I please push NOW!?" I screamed.

"Go ahead and push when you're ready," Dr. Sharon agreed.

After a few more pushes, he was here.

After he was out, I collapsed on back on the bed out of sheer exhaustion. Amy and my mom went to look at him and take pictures.

When they finally put him in my arms, I cried tears of joy. I counted every toe and finger and kissed his cute little nose over and over again. He was perfect.

Amy left to let my dad and Jake know and show them the pictures of the baby. After I was settled in my room, I finally ate again and dozed off to sleep.

I never heard from Isaiah the days I was in the hospital and I can't say I didn't care because I did. I did send him a picture the next morning. Although, I was glad the baby had his nose and mouth.

When Dr. Sharon came in I had her to perform the paternity test.

"Is the father coming in today so I can get his sample?" she asked.

"I'm not sure, but just in case go ahead and swab the baby." I told her.

She swabbed the baby and had the nurse take the sample to the lab. After the nurse left, she made sure I was feeling okay and healing fine.

I asked Amy to drive me home and when she came that afternoon, she had an officer on duty install the car seat for me before we left the hospital.

There was a knock on the door. I was only expecting Dr. Sharon and the nurses to visit today.

"Come in!" I yelled.

I was playing with the baby when I looked up to see Isaiah standing there.

"Hey, Zen," he said.

"Hey…" I replied. I'm surprised to see you. My doctor is ready to swab you when you're ready."

"So, that's lil man huh?" he asked walking towards the bed.

"Yep, in all of his glory," I said. Isn't he cute?"

"He is. He has my nose and my mouth," he said in amazement.

I was glad he could see his traits in the baby without my having to say it.

Dr. Sharon knocked and came into the room to make sure the baby was doing okay, before we headed out.

"Dr. Sharon, this is the baby's father. So, we can swab him now," I said.

"Hello and okay, I'll be right back," she said.

"This feels so. I don't know the word I'm looking for, but this doesn't feel right, doing this test. I'm looking at him and I see me," he said.

"I agree, but this is what you wanted. You guys needed the confirmation and we're about to get it," I said.

This hurt. I was choking back tears. Not, because I wanted him in my life, but this was ridiculous. Dr. Sharon came back into the room and swabbed Isaiah.

"Dr. Sharon, when will the results be back?" I asked.

"Let's give it about a week, just in case, and when the results come back, I'll give you a call."

"Okay, great. Thank you doctor," I said.

"Well, you two babies will be all set to go home in about an hour or so," Dr. Sharon said.

"Thanks," I said, smiling. We're going home, my "lil love."

Isaiah was smiling at the both of us.

"Do you mind if I hold him?" he asked, shyly.

"Nope, not at all." I said handing him the small package.

He sat in the chair across from me to hold him.

"Hey, 'lil guy. I'm your daddy," Isaiah said.

"So, what did you decide to name him?" he asked.

"Isaiah, meet your son, Robert Everette Smith," I said proudly.

"Oh…" he said.

"What is it?" I asked. You don't like the name?"

"I kinda thought he would have my last name," he said.

Really? Did he really think that? After all he's put me through these past few months?

"Wait. What? Why would you think that? We aren't married," I said.

"Is that what you want? Us to be married?" he asked.

"Nope. Not at all," I said. He's not going to have your last name."

"Can't we talk about this?" he asked.

"It's not up for discussion," I said, as I shrugged.

We sat in silence until Amy and Jake walked in. They were shocked to see Isaiah sitting there holding the baby. I was still in shock.

"Hey, guys! Wait. Jake, what are you doing here? I thought I was going to see you later tonight," I asked.

He stared at Isaiah with a cold look on his face.

"So, Isaiah, when did you get here?" Jake asked. Because you've been M.I.A. this whole time."

Oh, great. I did not need there to be any type of confrontation here at the hospital or anywhere else for that matter. I looked at Amy panicked.

"Guys, guys, let's not do this here; or anywhere," I said.

Amy stood beside Jake just in case he tried to lunge at him or something.

"I know I've been absent and I've apologized—to the one that matters," Isaiah said. "I'm here now and I'm all in and that's what matters."

"You have some nerve…" Jake said. Zen, I'll meet you guys at the house."

Jake stormed out of the hospital room.

"Do you mind if I come by later?" Isaiah asked.

"Isaiah, that may not be the best idea. There will be people there that are not happy with you, and I'm not filling my house with negativity," I said.

"I thought you said you wouldn't keep him from me?" Isaiah questioned, looking concerned.

"And I'm not. I said it's not a good idea to be around people who want your head on a platter. Trust me, this is for your own good."

Isaiah was still cuddling with the baby and stood up to give him back to me.

"Okay, I understand…" he said. I'll wait for you to call."

Straight No Chaser: The Beginning

He kissed the baby on the forehead and me on the cheek.

That took me—and Amy—by surprise.

"I'll be sure to call you," I said.

He disappeared behind the door. Amy looked at me with her eyes wide open.

"Whoa," she said.

"Yeah, I know, right? And no I didn't know he was coming today. Surprised us all," I said.

"Jake was about to whoop his behind!" Amy said laughing.

Dr. Sharon came back in and released us and had a nurse walk us all down to the car.

"Well, 'lil guy, say good-bye to your first room…" I said smiling.

On the way home all I could think about was our future. How I wanted the best for my baby. I loved this little guy more than I ever realized. He may have been conceived in a loveless relationship, but I would have more than enough love for him.

We finally made it home and my mom had invited some friends and family over. She also cooked a ginormous feast! I was hoping it was only going to be us, but I enjoyed the company.

Amy and Jake decided to spend the night and I am grateful. Robert gave us all a run for our money during the night.

Straight No Chaser: The Beginning

We were all zombies the next morning. Jake got up first and started brewing coffee. The smell of freshly brewed coffee woke me. When I woke up, the baby was still sleeping, thank goodness!

I walked into the kitchen and he had a cup already made for me.

"Oh my god, thank you!" I said.

"Good morning and you're welcome," he said laughing. Robert has some lungs on him!"

I laughed.

"Yeah, and just think you weren't even in the same room with him," I said laughing.

"I know! You want breakfast?" he asked.

I nodded as I sipped my coffee. I looked over and saw the stack of mail from the past few days.

"Thanks for getting the mail," I said.

"No prob," he said preparing breakfast.

I sat at the table looking through everything. I came across a manila envelope, and opened that first. As I read over the letter my face dropped and I yelled!

"Oh my god!!" I said, as I broke down crying.

Jake turned around and rushed over to the table. Amy was just walking into the kitchen.

"What's wrong?" Jake asked.

"Zen, baby, what's wrong?" Amy asked.

I looked at the both of them with tears streaming down my face.

"Isaiah and Keeley are suing me for full custody of Robert!"